U0728787

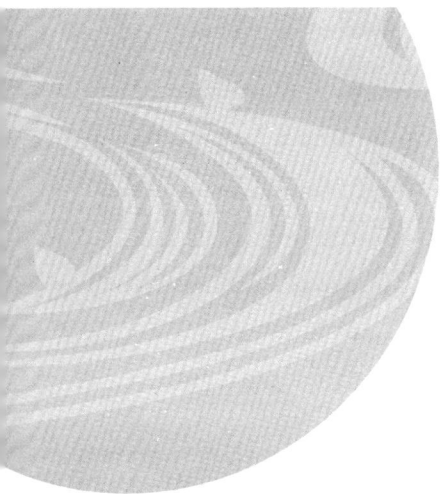

江雪：
中国唐宋诗词选

SNOW ON THE RIVER:
POEMS FROM THE TANG
AND SONG DYNASTIES OF CHINA

王守义　编选
Selected and Edited by
Wang Shouyi

王守义　约翰·诺弗尔　译
Translated by
Wang Shouyi and John Knoepfle

黑龙江大学出版社
HEILONGJIANG UNIVERSITY PRESS
哈尔滨

图书在版编目（CIP）数据

江雪：中国唐宋诗词选 / 王守义编选；王守义，
（美）约翰·诺弗尔（John Knoepfle）译 . -- 哈尔滨：
黑龙江大学出版社，2018.11（2022.10 重印）
ISBN 978-7-5686-0261-7

Ⅰ . ①江… Ⅱ . ①王… ②约… Ⅲ . ①唐诗－诗集－
汉、英②宋诗－诗集－汉、英③唐宋词－选集－汉、英
Ⅳ . ① I222.74 ② I222.84

中国版本图书馆 CIP 数据核字（2018）第 166587 号

江雪：中国唐宋诗词选
JIANGXUE:ZHONGGUO TANG SONG SHI CI XUAN
王守义　编选
王守义　约翰·诺弗尔　译

责任编辑　刘　双　侯天姣　张　慧
出版发行　黑龙江大学出版社
地　　址　哈尔滨市南岗区学府三道街 36 号
印　　刷　保定市铭泰达印刷有限公司
开　　本　880 毫米 ×1230 毫米　1/32
印　　张　11.5
字　　数　247 千
版　　次　2018 年 11 月第 1 版
印　　次　2022 年 10 月第 4 次印刷
书　　号　ISBN 978-7-5686-0261-7
定　　价　39.00 元

本书如有印装错误请与本社联系更换。

版权所有　侵权必究

物外山川近晴初

景靄深芳郊花草

遍何處不宜春

王守義教授惠存　癸酉仲冬溥任

溥任书写王勃的诗

溥任书写王勃的诗

物外山川近，
晴初景霭深。
芳郊花草遍，
何处不宜春。

癸酉仲冬

王守义教授惠存

书法：溥任

译者注：诗题《登城春望》，诗人王勃（唐），此版本来源于溥任的字幅。

Calligraphy of Wang Bo's Poem by
Pu Ren

beyond the place where I am standing

ranges and valleys seem closer to me

it is clearing now after the storm

scenes shrouded in mist remain far away

flowers everywhere scent the land in the suburbs

wherever you go spring will be there

The eleventh month in the lunar calendar, 1993

To Professor Wang Shouyi

Calligrapher: Pu Ren

Note from the translators: the title of the poem — *Up on the Gate Tower of the City in Spring* and the poet's name — Wang Bo (from the Tang Dynasty).

此照摄于 1995 年 9 月,美国伊利诺伊州春田市。

This photo was taken in Springfield, Illinois, USA in September, 1995.

作者简介

About the Authors

王守义于 1942 年生于中国辽宁省大连市,祖籍为山东省牟平县(现烟台市牟平区)。毕业于黑龙江大学英语语言文学专业,后在美国伊利诺伊大学完成美国文学专业硕士学位。

他曾为黑龙江大学学术委员会委员、英语系教授、美国文学专业研究生导师,曾担任英语系主任、美国研究所所长、外语学院副院长。

他曾于 1996 年至 1997 年应邀作为富布莱特驻美国学者(跨文化影响项目)任教于阿什兰大学英语系;后曾在伊利诺伊大学春田分校的国际研究中心任客座教授,在休斯敦大学亚裔美国人文化研究中心任客座研究员。

他曾任中国全国美国文学研究会副会长、中国跨文化交际学会常务理事、中国美国学学会理事、中国英语教学研究会理事、黑龙江省作家协会会员、《诗林》杂志特约编辑。

他曾以作者、合作者,译者、合译者,编者、合编者的身份在中国和美国出版十九本著作,包括他自己的诗集《风的愿望》。他曾撰写三十余篇论文,其中多篇发表在国家级学术刊物上,如《中国比较文学》《外国语》《外国文学评论》《求是学刊》《外语学刊》《文艺评论》《伊利诺伊评论》等。

他为七本出版著作撰写了序言,在中国、美国、韩国的研讨会上发表二十余篇论文。此外,他的多篇诗作、文艺杂谈、译诗、短篇小说翻译、书评见于多种报纸和刊物上。

他现在是加拿大文学翻译家协会顶级会员,与妻子孙苏荔住在加拿大橡树岭,与邦德湖和威尔考克斯湖为邻。夏天,他喜欢在湖上划他的独木舟 —— 湍流号;冬天,他喜欢在覆雪的山林小路上散步。

Wang Shouyi was born in Dalian City, Liaoning Province, China in 1942. His hometown is Muping County (now Muping District of Yantai City), Shandong Province, China. He graduated from Heilongjiang University with a major in English Language and Literature. Later he earned his Master Degree in American Literature at the University of Illinois Springfield (UIS).

At Heilongjiang University, he worked as a member of the Academic Committee of Heilongjiang University, a professor of the English department, an advisor for graduate students of American Literature, chairman of the English department, director of the Institute of American Studies and vice-dean of the Foreign Languages Institute .

As a Fulbright Professor in Residence in the USA on the Cross-Cultural Influence Program 1996−1997 , he taught in the English department, Ashland University, and later he served as a visiting professor teaching in the International Studies Centre at the UIS and also as a visiting researcher in the Asian American Cultural Studies Centre of University of Houston.

He was the vice-president of the China Association for the Study of American Literature, a standing council member of the China Association for Intercultural Communication, a council member of the China Association for American Studies, a council member of the China English Language Education Association. He was also a member of the Heilongjiang Writers Association and a special editor of the magazine

Poetry Forest.

His nineteen books have been published in China and the USA, of which he is as author or co-author, translator or co-translator, editor or co-editor. He also published the collection of his own poems — *The Wind's Will*. He has more than thirty essays, some of which appeared in nationally prestigious academic journals such as *Comparative Literature in China, Journal of Foreign Languages, Foreign Literature Review, Seeking Truth, Foreign Language Research, Literature and Art Criticism, Illinois Issues* and so on.

He also wrote seven prefaces for his and other authors' books. He has more than twenty papers presented at symposiums in China, the USA and South Korea. His poems, literary articles, translated poems, translated short stories and book reviews have been published in newspapers and magazines.

He is currently a full member of the Literary Translators' Association of Canada and lives with his wife Sun Suli at Oak Ridges close to Bond Lake and Lake Wilcox in Canada. He likes paddling his canoe "Speed River" in the lakes in summer and hiking on the snow-covered trails in the wooded hills in winter.

约翰·诺弗尔于 1923 年生于美国俄亥俄州辛辛那提市。二战期间,他服役于美国海军,在登陆艇部队任初级军官,在太平洋战争中曾运送第五海军陆战队登陆硫黄岛。在登岛作战时,他的双腿被弹片击中。伤愈后,他又参加运送二十二军登陆冲绳岛,伤势复发,军旅生涯结束。仍然存留在双腿里的炮弹碎片还能让他想起那个死里逃生的太平洋之夜。

1956 年,他结束了在辛辛那提的教育电视节目的工作,开始在俄亥俄州立大学、南伊利诺伊大学教英语。后来他又先后在玛丽维尔大学和圣路易斯大学担任英语和文学写作两门课的助教。从 1972 年到退休,他一直在伊利诺伊大学担任英国文学和文学写作教授。

他出版了约二十本诗集,其中包括《流入岛屿的河流》(芝加哥大学出版社,1965 年),《来自桑格蒙的诗》(伊利诺伊大学出版社,1985 年),《求赦免》(德瑞德出版社,1994 年),《抗饥荒的祈祷和其他爱尔兰诗歌》(堪萨斯市密苏里大学,BkMk 出版社,2004 年),《黄昏的芦荟》(印第安画笔诗人出版社,2015 年),还有各种学术论文和书评。1986 年,他曾因对中西部文学的杰出贡献获马克·吐温奖,同年获伊利诺伊年度优秀作家奖,2012 年在春田获市长艺术奖。

1985 年,他与王守义合作翻译了《唐诗选》和《宋诗词选》,由美国匙河诗歌出版社出版精装本和平装本,责任编辑是大卫·R.皮卡斯基。这两本书后于 1989 年由中国黑龙江人民出版社出版精装合订本《唐宋诗词英译》,责任编辑是李向东。他与王守义全力合作,每当完成共同满意的一行翻译,就会有成就感。约翰在翻译的过程中，对中国的诗歌、历史和文化产生了由衷的敬意。他还和罗伯特·布莱、詹姆斯·赖特合作翻译诗歌，出版了《凯撒·乌莱侯的二十首诗》。这些诗后来收进《聂鲁达和乌莱侯》一书中，由比肯出版社在 1971 年出版，此书在 1993 年再版。

他现在与妻子佩姬·诺弗尔住在伊利诺伊州春田市。他喜欢在一些场合给朋友和家人吹奏口琴。有时，在落雨的下午，他喜欢在电脑上尝试敲出几行好诗。

John Knoepfle was born in Cincinnati, Ohio, USA in 1923. He served in the Navy in World War Two as an officer in the Amphibious Corps, in the Pacific War, making assault landings for the 5th Marines at Iwo Jima and he was struck by a shell burst. After recovering, he joined the assault landing for the 22nd Army on Okinawa Island. But the injury reopened which ultimately brought an end to his military career. The shrapnel in his legs is still a reminder of his narrow escape that night in the Pacific.

In 1956 his educational television career in Cincinnati ended and he began his career as an instructor in English at Ohio State University and Southern Illinois University. He served as an assistant professor of English and Creative Writing at Maryville University and later at Saint Louis University. From 1972 until his retirement, he was a professor of

English Literature and Creative Writing at the University of Illinois Springfield.

He has published some twenty books of poems including *Rivers into Islands* (University of Chicago Press, 1965), *Poems from the Sangamon* (University of Illinois Press, 1985), *Begging an Amnesty* (The Druid Press, 1994), *Prayer Against Famine and other Irish Poems* (BkMk Press, University of Missouri, Kansas City, 2004)and *The Aloe of Evening* (Indian Paintbrush Poets, 2015). Awards include the Mark Twain Award for Distinguished Contributions to Midwestern Literature in 1986, Illinois Excellent Author of the Year in 1986, Mayor's Awards for the Arts, in Springfield in 2012.

He began working together with Wang Shouyi and published the translations of *Tang Dynasty Poems* and *Song Dynasty Poems* in hardback and paperback which were published by Spoon River Poetry Press in 1985, David R. Pichaske was the editor. These books were combined into one — *Poems from Tang and Song Dynasties* in hardback in 1989 which was published by Heilongjiang People's Publishing House, Li Xiangdong was the editor. John and Shouyi shared hard work and a sense of achievement whenever they agreed on a good line. And John gained a serious respect for Chinese poetry, history and culture. He also translated poems with Robert Bly and James Wright and published in the book *Twenty Poems of Cesar Vallejo*. Those poems were reprinted in *Neruda and Vallejo* by Beacon Press in 1971 and republished in 1993.

He lives with his wife Peggy Knoepfle in Springfield, Illinois. He enjoys playing the harmonica for friends and family on occasion. And sometimes he likes to try striking a few good lines on his computer on a rainy afternoon.

前　言

　　黑龙江大学出版社在决定出版由我编选,由我与美国著名诗人约翰·诺弗尔合作翻译的《归舟:中国元明清诗选》的同时,又决定出版由我编选,由我与美国著名诗人约翰·诺弗尔合作翻译的《江雪:中国唐宋诗词选》,以形成系列。望能充分展示中国古典诗歌在唐、宋、元、明、清五个朝代中,从兴起到衰落的完整的演变历程,把这一片群星璀璨的历史文化的天空,呈现给全世界读者。

　　《江雪:中国唐宋诗词选》里收进的诗词是来自我与美国著名诗人约翰·诺弗尔合作翻译的《唐诗选》和《宋诗词选》,以及《唐宋诗词英译》。《唐诗选》和《宋诗词选》由美国匙河诗歌出版社于1985年以精装和平装两种形式印刷出版,《唐宋诗词英译》由黑龙江人民出版社于1989年以精装本印刷出版。《江雪:中国唐宋诗词选》包括唐诗七十三首,选自三十八位诗人;宋诗三十四首,选自二十二位诗人;宋词二十一首,选自十一位词人。诗人和词人时有重叠。

　　由美国匙河诗歌出版社出版的两本书均由美国伊利诺伊州艺术委员会和美国国家艺术支援会赞助出版,当时没有加中文书名。芝加哥艺术博物院为这两本书提供了罗伯特·艾勒顿收藏的一幅中国画家朱伦瀚（1680—1760）的山水画，作为两本书的封面。三十年过去了，亚马逊网站上仍然会出现将译本作为收藏品的交易。

由黑龙江人民出版社出版的《唐宋诗词英译》在国内发行后，黑龙江省翻译工作者协会与《外语学刊》编辑部邀请省内著名学者、教授、翻译家举行了学术讨论会，研讨这本译诗集以及其中收为附录的论文《论中国古诗词英译》，会后由学刊编辑王德庆先生执笔发表了综合报道《一次关于中国古诗词英译的讨论》，介绍了各位与会专家的评论及分析（《外语学刊》，1992 年 03 期）。同期还刊登了著名教授李锡胤先生的长篇书面发言《从李清照〈如梦令〉英译文谈起——在哈尔滨王守义、诺弗尔〈唐宋诗词英译讨论会〉上的发言》。李锡胤教授以大学者的风范拿出自己以格律体翻译英诗的尝试，做了举证论述。著名翻译家赵辛而先生最早撰写了论文《从两部英译古诗集看近年来古诗英译之趋势》（《外语学刊》，1986 年 04 期），对美国版本的两本译书（当时尚没有在国内出版合订修订版）进行了详尽的缕析，与国内外中国古典诗歌翻译界的各种见解多有比照和评述，还列举了卞之琳、吕叔湘、翁显良、许渊冲、丰华瞻等译家见解。后来又见到南开大学外语学院陆林教授对《唐宋诗词英译》里的一些译诗与许渊冲教授的翻译进行的比较研究《诗歌翻译别是一家——〈枫桥夜泊〉等唐诗的两种译文比较》（崔永禄主编，《高等院校英语专业翻译实践和鉴赏教程：文学翻译佳作对比赏析》，南开大学出版社，2001 年，2006 年再版）。当然近年来还有很多论文、著述对我和约翰·诺弗尔翻译的唐宋诗词进行分析研究与评论，以及对附录中我撰写的论文《论中国古诗词英译》广泛地引用分析和探讨。其中辽宁对外经贸学院李国超教授,特别从文学翻译的角度对译诗和论文进行了探讨(《文学翻译中的文学思潮刍议》,《赤峰学院学报(汉文哲学社会科学版)》,2016年01期)。令人肃然起敬的是,这些论述不但评论、研究了这本译著,更对古诗词英译这一整体进行了深入探讨,看出事关中国文化。我和约翰·诺弗尔教授为此深感兴奋,深受鼓舞,深知自己不是寂寞的译家。

这次出版《江雪:中国唐宋诗词选》没有增加译诗,但是做了若干修订,订正了许多在旧版中出现的印刷错误。对译诗有较多修订,其中几首有较大改动,字句多有斟酌。旧版本中收入了《论中国古诗词英译》作为附录,新版中保留了这篇论文,作为后记,并对这篇论文进行了较大幅度的修改,考虑到篇幅,删掉了五首引用的译诗,但是论文所讨论的观点基本没有改动。这并非因为原论文已经被广泛引用,而是觉得那些三十年前的讨论,在当今仍然有现实的学术意义。原论文是我在美国翻译唐宋诗词过程中,对一些中国古诗词英译的思考和在翻译时对所做出的选择的思考。1987年12月,我应邀参加在香港举行的当代翻译国际研讨会,该论文作为入选论文在会上宣读。之后,在上海外国语学院(现为上海外国语大学)学报《外国语》上,以《中国古诗词英译刍议》为题发表了这篇论文(《外国语》,1988年04期)。

《江雪:中国唐宋诗词选》,题目中的"江雪"是来自本书中唐朝诗人柳宗元的一首诗的题目——《江雪》。本书是一本诗词作品的选集，是文学作品，选其中一首诗的题目作为本书题目的一部分，一定会使读者更加浮想联翩，至少译者已经为此而沉思不已。我每次背诵柳宗元这首《江雪》时，在享受陶醉之余，总会陷入沉思。冥想之中常常会认定，中华文化基因的密码很可能就在这首诗里。只是它太深邃，我从未达到顿悟。我自知不如《达·芬奇密码》影片中，好莱坞明星汉克斯扮演的教授那么幸运，只费了一些周折，就破解了密码。我常想，柳宗元在一千二百多年前，写出这句"独钓寒江雪"，并非只说雪落寒江，蓑翁独钓。千年来人们也都只说，孤舟上的蓑翁在钓鱼。没有人说他是在钓雪。我在翻译这首诗时，也沿用了这个思路。其实柳宗元这首诗蕴含的无限禅意，正在于其"钓雪"的暗示：雪非鱼，入水即融。这首诗的空灵、神韵、意境、禅思、天人融溶，表现出中国唐宋诗词的境界真谛，经千年剥析，仍然神秘如初。《江雪》那时就实现了二十世纪后半期西方文学批评中所追求的写出五度空间。

在这次出版的《江雪：中国唐宋诗词选》中，译者为部分译诗增加了注释，与同时出版的《归舟：中国元明清诗选》统一起来。因为后者，在翻译的过程中，正值互联网的兴起，只要注释出关键的内容或者关键的词语，读者借助互联网就能很快地查到全面的信息。这样一来，在中国古诗词英译时，添加注释就成为可能，否则译诗将被淹没在注释的汪洋大海之中。尽管如此，译者在翻译过程中还是争取让读者在不读注释的情况下，就能理解诗意、诗的文化内涵，产生诗的震撼、情绪的感应，实现接受主体进行诗的再创造。书中只针对地理、历史、文化典故等可能会带来理解障碍的词语进行了注释，而不涉及任何关于诗词的解读诠释,把艺术欣赏的殿堂留给伟大的读者。考虑到读者可能在某一瞬间打开本书的某一页,只阅读某一首诗,所以在需要注释的部分,我也毫不犹豫地重复地对其进行了注释。让读者免去查找之烦,能静心欣赏。书中没有提供诗词的中文注释,因为我认为,有兴趣读这些古诗词和古诗词英译,并且母语又是中文的读者,不需要中文注释帮助了解诗词中的历史、地理与文化背景。书中的英文注释是为母语是英语的读者准备的。

同时,根据诗人的生卒年,重新调整了书中诗词的先后排序。距离旧版的出版时间,已有二十多年,现今很多诗人的生卒年份已经得到确认。书中对诗人排序奉行的原则还是出生早的排在前,如果出生年相同,卒年早的在前,生卒年均不详的,排在最后,下次再版时,如果能确认生卒年份,再做调整。这样的排序有助于读者感受到,在时代的变迁中,诗人的命运和创作,以及中国古典诗歌在历史的沿革中起伏跌宕的发展脉络。

本书中,诗词的选择照顾到知名诗人和脍炙人口的诗词作品,也照顾到年代、地域、题材、体裁、流派等方面。收集的诗词涉及朝廷、战争、农耕、行商、交通、仕途、疾病、别离、友谊、爱情、家庭及人的追求。既写到帝王侯门也写到普通百姓;既写到痛苦灾难也写到美好生活;既写到市井乡村也写到田园自然。所选的诗词是由各个历史朝代里不甘寂寞的个体书写的,在个体不可控制的大环境中,其人生或精彩纷呈,或潦倒困顿,或斑斓多变。选择永远是困难的。可是我对这些诗词的选择却相对容易一些,我的早已谢世的祖父帮了大忙,因为他当年教我的诗词大多入选。在我还没有入小学时,家住青岛贵州路海边的一栋二层楼上,站在面向大海一侧的明走廊上，看涨潮时海水怎样漫过后院的柳条篱笆墙根。祖父几乎每天都要坐在床沿上，一只手拉着我的手，另一只手拉着弟弟的手，爷孙三人一齐左右摇晃，伴随有节奏的海涛声，背诵唐宋诗词。高兴了，甚至吟唱那些五言和七言的诗，我至今仍能用祖父教的音调吟唱那些诗。当时只知诗的大意，可是至今不忘，仍然记得那些诗、祖父和弟弟。这就是中华文化的魅力，这就是中华人文传承的基因。也许基因的密码真的就在这些诗里。

也正是源于此，我的选择原则是不回避难于翻译的诗词，而且越是难的越要选。所谓难，就是诗中的典故多，包括历史、地理、政治、宗教、传说、神话、民间故事，甚至对其他文学作品的参照。中国是一个历史悠久、文化深远、传统绵延、文学博大的国家，所有用于诗中的典故，往往都具有十分厚重的文化内涵。翻译好这些典故，才能在把中国古典诗词传扬至海外的同时，弘扬中国传统文化。我曾有一次在香港华语诗人作家座谈会上发言，并提出一个口号："我们走向世界，世界走向我们。"读者会看到，在本书所选的诗词中，重复出现牛郎织女、寒食清明、重阳中秋、钱塘江潮、庙宇神明、长河大漠、高山浩湖等等典故，希望这些意象和神话融入外国文化之中，架起文化沟通之桥，促进不同文化的互动，不会像牛郎织女那么辛苦。从翻译的角度看，处理好这些用典，把握住可译与不可译之间的分寸，选择两种不同文化的连接点，让诗意和诗的文化精髓去飨宴读者，也是中国古典诗歌英译的更上一层楼。

在宋词的选择中，所选多有篇幅大、卷帙浩繁、通篇用典、典出幽邃、境界不同凡响的名篇。越是爱不释手，越是下笔维艰，致使译者夜不能寐，时而有之；力作不能不选，然而力作就愈要译者的功力，致使译者食不甘味，时而有之。我至今仍为选了那些难以翻译的宋词感到高兴，因为它们确实具有强大的文化冲撞力。王国维先生在《人间词话》中，高论成大业者必经的三个境界时，分别引用了三首词中的诗句，我尤其为自己选择翻译了这三首词而感到欣慰。从少年时代起，这三个境界的意象一直萦绕脑际。经多年琢磨，我始终不能想象出，王国维先生是怎样从爱意缠绵、离愁别绪、寻寻觅觅的爱情诗词中，找出象征成大业的人生必经的三个境界的。第一境界："昨夜西风凋碧树，独上高楼，望尽天涯路。"（晏殊《蝶恋花》）第二境界："衣带渐宽终不悔，为伊消得人憔悴。"（柳永《蝶恋花》）第三境界："众里寻他千百度，蓦然回首，那人却在，灯火阑珊处。"（辛弃疾《青玉案·元夕》）特别是第三境界，王国维先生将其升华为"内外圆融而顿悟"。真乃大家，一语破的，让词家瞠目，让禅家结舌。我是从王国维先生那里知道，诗词是可以这样读的，而且诗词里的意象和象征的文化凝聚力，不可估量。我说这些，只是庆幸我没有知难而退，而是把这三首词翻译入选。

作为插页收入本书中的书法字幅是出自中国著名国画家、书法家溥任先生（1918—2015）的手笔。字幅写的是唐朝诗人王勃（650?—676?）的诗《登城春望》，后附有我与约翰对这首诗的英文翻译，等于王勃的诗也收入在选集里，只是没有列入目录。自从我收到这份礼物，我就想找机会把他印在我的书里，以便让更多的读者有机会欣赏这精湛的艺术品。现在终于如愿以偿了。溥任先生的祖母是慈禧太后，伯父是光绪皇帝，哥哥是宣统皇帝。他一生安于清贫，为社会、为教育、为艺术奉献自己的一生和自己拥有的一切。溥任先生三年前谢世，把他的这幅字收在这本书里，也是对溥任先生的纪念。

这本《江雪：中国唐宋诗词选》能够顺利出版，与《归舟：中国元明清诗选》形成系列，我和约翰·诺弗尔都十分感谢黑龙江大学出版社，特别感谢总编辑刘剑刚先生的眼光、耐心和支持。

感谢刘双编辑的热忱关切、认真负责和全力帮助。

感谢徐文培教授的学术支持和不倦地关心。

感谢洛赞妮·福莱特女士和宜森·兰姆先生。感谢他们在校对中提供的帮助和建议。

我和约翰·诺弗尔要特别向佩姬·诺弗尔女士和孙苏荔女士致谢，感谢她们在该书出版的长期准备工作中所给予的全程支持、关心及帮助。

虽然借这次出版机会得以修订以前在印刷中出现的错误，但是由于编译者水平所限，错漏之处，亦恐难免。如蒙同好不吝指正，将不胜感激，愿与共勉。

王守义

2018 年 8 月

于多伦多教堂街

Preface

In order to have a set of books that displays the full course of Chinese classical poetry from its rise to decline through five dynasties: the Tang, Song, Yuan, Ming and Qing dynasties, Heilongjiang University Press decided to publish the following two books, *Snow on the River: Poems from the Tang and Song Dynasties of China* and *Voyage Home: Poems from the Yuan and Ming and Qing Dynasties of China*, selected and edited by Wang Shouyi and translated by Wang Shouyi and John Knoepfle, a well-known American poet. The purpose is to present the historical Chinese culture like skies with clusters of twinkling stars to readers all over the world.

The poems selected for *Snow on the River: Poems from the Tang and Song Dynasties of China* are from the following two books: *The Tang Dynasty Poems* and *The Song Dynasty Poems*, which were a collaboration in translation by John Knoepfle and I, were published in paperback and hardback by Spoon River Poetry Press in America in 1985. And the poems are also from the book:

Poems from the Tang and Song Dynasties which was a combination of the previous two books with some new translations added and was published in hardback by Heilongjiang People's Publishing House in China in 1989. Among these selected poems in this book there are seventy-three poems from thirty-eight poets in the Tang Dynasty and thirty-four poems from twenty-two poets in the Song Dynasty as well as twenty-one lyrics for traditional melodies from eleven lyric writers in the Song Dynasty. It was common then that lyric writers were also poets.

The two anthologies published by Spoon River Poetry Press were printed in part with funds provided by the Illinois Arts Council, a state organization, and by the National Endowment for the Arts. There were no titles in Chinese for the books printed then. The painting on book cover — *Landscape* by Zhu Lunhan (1680–1760) was from Robert Allerton Collection of The Art Institute of Chicago. After thirty years I still see the books advertised on Amazon as collectables.

After *Poems from the Tang and Song Dynasties* published by Heilongjiang People's Publishing House became available in the book market in China, Heilongjiang Translators Association and the editorial board of the journal, *Foreign Language Research* jointly invited well-known scholars, professors and translators to their symposium reviewing this anthology of Chinese classical poems and the essay "On the Translation of Chinese Classical Poems into

English" which was included in the book. Later, Mr. Wang Deqing from the editorial board wrote a comprehensive dispatch "The Academic Deliberation Report: A Discussion on the Translation of Chinese Classical Poems" introducing the reviews and analyses from the experts at the symposium (*Foreign Language Research*, 3rd Issue, 1992). Also appearing in the same issue was the prestigious professor Li Xiyin's written speech "Comments on the English Translation of Li Qingzhao's Lyric *Rumengling* — a Speech at the Symposium on the Book — *Poems from the Tang and Song Dynasties* Translated by Wang Shouyi and John Knoepfle" (*Foreign Language Research*, 3rd Issue, 1992). Li Xiyin as a great scholar attempted to prove his perception by showing his own practice of translating an English poem into Chinese using the traditional Chinese poetry form. Distinguished translator Mr. Zhao Xiner is the earliest one to write a paper on those two books as there was no combined version available then "Review of the Trend in Translating Chinese Classical Poems into English from Reading Two Anthologies." (*Foreign Language Research*, 4th Issue, 1986) He detailed his analyses and made a careful comparison between the points of view regarding the art of translation, specifically focusing on the viewpoints on translation of Chinese classical poems into English from translators and critics in China and abroad including Bian Zhilin, Lü Shuxiang, Weng Xianliang, Xu Yuanchong and Feng Huazhan. Later I came across a paper of comparative study between poems in this book and in Xu Yuanchong's, titled "Translation of Poems with Unique Style — Comparison between Two Types of Translations regarding *Anchored at Night near Maple Bridge* and Other Poems" by Lu Lin, professor at College of Foreign Language of Nankai University (Cui Yonglu, *A Course in Practice and Appreciation of Translation for English Department in Higher Education: Compare and Review Excellent Works in Literary Translation,* Nankai University Press in 2001, reprinted in 2006). In recent years there have been more papers and books of reviews and comments on the translations of poems from the Tang and Song dynasties by John Knoepfle and myself. And the paper I wrote "On the Translation of Chinese Classical Poems into English" has been quoted in many different papers. Among all the responses and remarks Li Guochao, professor at Liaoning University of International Business and Economics, in his paper "A Modest Proposal to the Trends of Literary Thought in Literary Translation" reviewed and discussed both the translation and the essay in the book (*Journal of Chifeng University, Philosophy and Social Science Chinese Edition,* 2016). All these writings not only explore and review our translations but also further explore the whole cause of translating Chinese classical poems into English. This is respectful. I know this is related to Chinese culture. John and I feel so happy, so inspired, and so aware that we are not lonely translators.

We made quite a few revisions, particularly corrections on those errors in printing but we didn't add any new translations in this edition. More revisions were made to translations, trying to weigh a bit more on selection of words in some lines, and more changes were made in a number of translated poems. In the last edition, the article "On the Translation of Chinese Classical Poems into English" was included as an appendix, which is still kept in this edition but as the epilogue and is greatly revised. In order to make it shorter I deleted the five quoted poems but the viewpoints were not changed at all. This is not because the article has been quoted so much but I have a feeling that the discussions taking place thirty years ago are still having academic value. It is about my thoughts in the process of translating poems from the Tang and Song dynasties regarding translation of Chinese classical poems into English, especially about the thoughts of making choices while translating. In December, 1987, I was invited to the International Conference on Today's Translation held in Hong Kong to present this article. Later, the article was published by *Journal of Foreign Languages*, journal of Shanghai Foreign Languages Institute (now Shanghai International Studies University) titled "The Modest Suggestion on the Translation of Chinese Classical Poems into English" (*Journal of Foreign Languages*, 4th Issue, 1988).

"Snow on the River" in the title of this book is selected from Liu Zongyuan's poem *Snow on the River*, which is included in this anthology. As an anthology of poetry, a literary work, it will present readers with throngs of ideas, at least I myself have been thinking all the time. I fall into deep thoughts every time I recite Liu Zongyuan's poem *Snow on the River* and enjoy it. Very often, while racking my mind I begin to feel that the code of the Chinese culture gene may very possibly be present in this poem. However, the truth is just too abstruse and profound for me to get the sudden enlightenment. I know I would never be as lucky as the professor played by Hollywood star Tom Hanks in the film *The Da Vinci Code*, who solved the code just after a few ups and downs. I often think of this verse line written by Liu Zongyuan more than one thousand two hundred years ago: "who sits on deck and fishes by himself / where the snow falls on the cold water," which does not only mean: "Snow falls on the cold water and a fisherman in straw rain cape is fishing alone." But it has been a thousand years that the line is still interpreted as "the fisherman in straw rain cape is fishing alone on the only boat," which is exactly what I followed in our translation. Nobody has ever said the fisherman is fishing snow. In fact, the profound mood of Zen Buddhism implied in this poem by Liu Zongyuan originates in the hint of fishing snow: snow is not fish and melts instantly in water. The void, charm, mood, mind of Zen Buddhism, fusion of nature and human being are representing the essence of the ideal state in the poems in the Tang and Song dynasties of China, which is still as mysterious as when it came into being — after being interpreted for over a thousand years. Even at that time *Snow on the River* must have reached that five-dimensional space sought after in western literary criticism in the late twentieth century.

Notes were added to the translations of some poems in this edition in accordance with the other book published at the same time — *Voyage Home: Poems from the Yuan and Ming and Qing Dynasties of China.* When we started the translation of the second book we knew we could put a limited number of simple notes to the key words or the key content as readers could easily access on the Internet and obtain all the information they needed. Thus it becomes possible to add short and simple notes to the translation of Chinese classical poems, otherwise the translation could be flooded by an ocean of notes. Even though we can add notes we tried our best to make it possible for readers, before reading these notes, to comprehend the poetic flavor, understand cultural implication, get the poetic shock, react emotionally and further to participate in the recreation as the receptive subject. Notes are limited to and focused on understanding the obstacles caused by geography, history, cultural allusions, but they do not touch anything related to interpretation and explanation of the poem. The temple hall of art appreciation is reserved for our respected readers. Under the assumption that a reader may open the anthology to any page at any moment to read just one poem on that page I never hesitate to add a duplicate note thinking this will help a reader to avoid troubling looking for a note on some other page but to enjoy the reading without any disturbances. There are no notes in Chinese language provided because I believe Chinese native speakers who are interested in reading Chinese classical poems and the English translations of these poems will not need help to know the historical, geographical and caltural backgrounds in these poems. Notes in English in this book are supposed to help English-speaking readers.

Meanwhile, the chronological sequence of poets' appearing in this book has been rearranged. In the past twenty years researchers have found information about the years of birth and death for several poets that was not available before. This is the reason why the order was changed and is different from the old editions. The principle for chronological sequence in this book is still the same as before. Those who were born earlier appear ahead, but if they were born in the same year, those who passed away earlier appear ahead. If there is no information about either year of birth or year of death for a poet, the poet was arranged in the end of the book waiting for adjustment when information is available in the next edition. This chronological sequence will help readers feel the pulse of the fate and writing of poets in changing times and also the ups and downs that Chinese classical poetry went through along with the historical changes.

The intension of selecting poets and poems in this book is to present both well-known poets and popular poems with attention to times, locations, themes, types and schools of style. Poems selected are relating to imperial courts, wars, farming, trade, transportation, official careers, diseases, farewell, friendship, love, family and dreams of human beings. What they depict is not only about emperors and aristocrats but also common people; and not only about sorrows and disasters but also beauty and happy life; and not only about town and country but also land and gardens in nature. The selected poems, written by those individuals in every historical dynasty who hated to be overlooked in an environment that was out of control of individuals, are full of wonders or miserably hopeless or splendid but full of setbacks. It is always hard to select. But it is not that difficult for me to select these poems because I got great help from my Grandfather who passed away many years ago though. He taught me a lot of poems, most of which were selected for this book. Before I entered primary school my family lived on the second floor of a building right on the seashore in Guizhou Street in Qingdao. Standing in the open corridor facing the sea, I could see how waves crawl up and over the roots of the willow branch fence when the tide came in. Grandpa sat at the edge of the bed with my younger brother and me on each side, holding hands with us. We swayed together from side to side reciting poems and lyrics from the Tang and Song dynasties in accordance with wave rhythm of the sea we could hear. Sometimes we got excited singing those poems of five words to a line or poems of seven words to a line. Now I can still sing those poems with the tune taught by Grandpa. I could only understand the gist of those poems then, but I can remember them now. I remember the poems, my Grandpa and my younger brother. This is the fascination of Chinese culture and this is the gene inherited through generations. Maybe the code of the gene is really in these poems.

Therefore I never tried to avoid difficult poems in my selection for translation. On the contrary, I intended to select those difficult ones. To classify poems as difficult we usually indicate those with a lot more allusions originating in history, geography, politics, religion, legends, mythology, folklore tales and acquisitions of quotations from other literary works. China is a country of long history, profound and long-lasting culture, far-reaching tradition, broad and extensive literature so that the allusions used in poems generally carry a very heavy load of culture. Unless allusions are well-handled Chinese classical poems won't be able to travel abroad, to carry forward Chinese traditional culture and to accelerate cognition to Chinese culture. I raised the flag that "We go out to the world and in return the world comes to us" at the symposium of poets and writers of the Chinese language in Hong Kong in 1987. I'm sure readers of this book will see from selected poems the repeated acquisitions of allusions as Cowherd and Fairy Maiden (Altair and Vega), Cold Food Day, Qingming Festival, Chongyang Festival (the Ninth Day of the Ninth Month in the Lunar Calendar), Mid-Autumn Festival (The Moon Festival), the tide at the mouth of Qiantang River, temple and god, long river and vast desert, high mountains and huge lakes and their related stories. Hopefully these images and mythology will be absorbed into foreign cultures to build a bridge for connecting cultures, which will make the interactions between people in different cultures much easier than the reunion between Cowherd and Fairy Maiden. From the angle of translation dealing with allusions well, handling the space between the impossible for translation and the possible for translation well, selecting the connecting point between two cultures, offering readers the mood and cultural essence of poems will further upgrade the art of translating Chinese classical poems into English.

In the selection of lyrics to traditional melodies in the Song Dynasty most of them are long, complicated, full of allusions from great sources and outstanding in the state of mind attained. The poems you feel harder to give up are more difficult to translate. That's why sometimes I can't sleep at night. Masterpieces have to be selected but masterpieces require more talent and efforts from a translator. That's why sometimes I can't enjoy a good meal. I'm especially satisfied with the decision I made to select those difficult lyrics to traditional melodies because they really have the strength to produce very powerful breakthroughs in cultural fusion. I'm specially satisfied with my selection of three lyrics, from which Wang Guowei (1877–1927) selected some lines to illustrate the three phases a man of great success has to struggle through in his *Reviews on Lyrics to Traditional Melodies*. Since my early youth the images of the three phases have hunted my mind. After so many years of pondering I'm still wondering how Wang Guowei illuminated those lines from three lyrics of lingering love, sadness of parting and looking for and seeking after love to symbolize the three phases a man of great success must experience. Phase one: the wind out of the west / withered the green trees last night / now I climb alone / to the upper story of this house / and watch the road leading to the horizon (Yan Shu, *Lines for the Dielianhua Melody*); phase two: I feel my clothes are getting baggier / I look more and more wan and pallid / but I don't regret missing her badly / it's worth looking haggard / for a woman you love (Liu Yong, *Lines for the Dielianhua Melody*); phase three: and I look for her all through the festival / a hundred times until suddenly I glanced back / and saw where she stood alone in that place / where one or two lanterns still burned (Xin Qiji, *Lines for the Qingyu'an Melody: the Lantern Festival*). (All translations quoted above are from this book.) Particularly for the third phase, Wang Guowei sublimated it as "Sudden enlightenment with harmonious fusion of the inside and the outside." The sublimation from the great man of letters is right to the point, which makes the lyric writers stare and Zen Buddhists speechless. I learned from Wang Guowei that I can read lyrics that way and discover the tremendous power of culture. We didn't retreat from difficulties. Instead, we translated the three pieces of lyrics and selected them for this anthology.

The calligraphy as an insertion in this book is by Pu Ren (1918– 2015), a well-known Chinese artist who specialized in Chinese traditional painting and calligraphy. Pu Ren wrote in the vertical scroll a poem from Wang Bo (650? – 676?), a poet of the Tang Dynasty, which is titled *Up on the Gate Tower of the City in Spring*. Along with the insertion is the English translation of the poem by Wang Shouyi and John Knoepfle. I'm glad this poem from Wang Bo can be considered as selected for this anthology, it is not listed in the content though. As soon as I received this gift I made up my mind to print it in my book so that more readers can have the opportunity to enjoy the fine arts. Now the dream has come true. Although his Grandma was Empress Dowager Cixi, his Uncle was Emperor Guangxu and his elder brother was Emperor Xuantong he was willing to live a life of scanty means and determined to contribute to society, to set up and run a school for children and to serve the muse with all respect by offering his life and all the means he had. As Mr. Pu Ren passed away three years ago, this calligraphy as an insertion in this anthology could serve also as a commemoration.

John Knoepfle and I extend our thanks to Heilongjiang University Press and especially to Mr. Liu Jiangang, the chief editor, for his judgement and action, patience and support, which made it possible for *Snow on the River: Poems from the Tang and Song Dynasties of China* and *Voyage Home: Poems from the Yuan and Ming and Qing Dynasties of China* to be published at the same time and to form a set.

Many thanks go to Ms. Liu Shuang, editor, for her sincere care, kind consideration, and conscientious help.

We are indebted to Professor Xu Wenpei for his academic support and tireless care.

We owe our thanks to Ms. Rozanne Flatt and Mr. Ethan Lam for their help and suggestions in proofreading.

John Knoepfle and I are so grateful to Mrs. Peggy Knoepfle and Ms. Sun Suli for their constant and ever-lasting support, encouragement and help in years of preparation for the book.

This is a great opportunity for us to correct all the errors in printing in the previous edition. However due to the limitation of my ability, there will be mistakes inevitably. We hope getting suggestions and corrections from our readers and we'll feel grateful and encouraged to receive them.

Wang Shouyi
August, 2018
Church Street, Toronto
Translated by Amy Shiying Lam, revised by Wang Shouyi

目录·Contents

唐朝诗选
The Tang Dynasty Poems
618—907

贺知章 He Zhizhang (659—744?)

回乡偶书 ·· 2

A Few Lines after Returning to My Hometown ···················· 3

张 旭 Zhang Xu (675?—750?)

桃花溪 ·· 4

Mountain River with Peach Blossoms ···························· 5

王 翰 Wang Han (687—726)

凉州词 ·· 6

Liangzhou Song ·· 7

王之涣 Wang Zhihuan (688—742)

登鹳雀楼 ·· 8

Climbing the Stork Kiosk ···························· 9

凉州词 ·· 10

Liangzhou Song ······································· 11

孟浩然 Meng Haoran (689—740)

春 晓 ·· 12

At Dawn in Spring ···································· 13

宿建德江 ·· 14

Anchored at Night on the River in Jiande City ········· 15

王昌龄 Wang Changling (698—756?)

从军行 ·· 16

Border Duty ·· 17

出 塞 ·· 18

Beyond the Border ···································· 19

闺 怨 ·· 20

Bride's Complaint ···································· 21

王 维 Wang Wei (701?—761)

九月九日忆山东兄弟 ································· 22

The Ninth Day of the Ninth Month in the Lunar Calendar

I think of My Brothers on the East Side

of the Mountain ·································· 23

渭城曲 ·················· 24

Wei City Song ·················· 25

李　白 Li Bai（701—762）

静夜思 ·················· 26

Thoughts on a Quiet Evening ·················· 27

秋浦歌（之十四） ·················· 28

Qiupu Song (No. 14) ·················· 29

陪侍郎叔游洞庭醉后 ·················· 30

Li Bai Accompanied His Uncle on a Visit to Dongting Lake

and Wrote this Poem after Getting Drunk ·················· 31

峨眉山月歌 ·················· 32

Song of the Moon on Mount Emei ·················· 33

望庐山瀑布 ·················· 34

Watching the Lushan Mountain Falls ·················· 35

望天门山 ·················· 36

View of Tianmenshan Mountain ·················· 37

赠汪伦 ·················· 38

To Wang Lun ·················· 39

春夜洛城闻笛 ·················· 40

Lines while Hearing a Flute Playing

One Spring Night in Luo City ·················· 41

黄鹤楼送孟浩然之广陵 ·················· 42

Seeing Meng Haoran off ·················· 43

早发白帝城 ··· 44

Leaving Baidi City in the Early Morning ···················· 45

刘长卿 Liu Changqing (709?—786?)

逢雪宿芙蓉山主人 ·· 46

Taken in for the Night in My Host's House on Lotus Mountain

When I Was Caught in the Snow ····························· 47

杜　甫 Du Fu (712—770)

江畔独步寻花 ··· 48

Alone and Looking for Flowers on the River Bank ··········· 49

赠花卿 ·· 50

Song for Hua the Mighty General ···························· 51

绝　句 ·· 52

Jueju — a Four-line Poem with Seven Words to a Line ······ 53

绝　句 ·· 54

Jueju — a Four-line Poem with Five Words to a Line ········ 55

八阵图 ·· 56

The Eight Battle Formations ································· 57

江南逢李龟年 ··· 58

Meeting Li Guinian in the South of the Yangtze River ········ 59

岑　参 Cen Shen (715?—770)

逢人京使 ………………………………………… 60

Meeting the Envoy on His Way to the Capital ……… 61

张　继 Zhang Ji (715?—779?)

枫桥夜泊 ………………………………………… 62

Anchored at Night near Maple Bridge ……………… 63

韦应物 Wei Yingwu (737—792)

滁州西涧 ………………………………………… 64

The Western Ravine in Chuzhou …………………… 65

李　端 Li Duan (737?—784?)

听　筝 …………………………………………… 66

Listening to Zither Playing ………………………… 67

戎　昱 Rong Yu (744—800)

塞上曲 …………………………………………… 68

Border Ballad ……………………………………… 69

卢　纶 Lu Lun (748?—800?)

和张仆射塞下曲 (之二) ………………………… 70

Reply to Zhang Puye's Border Song (*No. 2*) ……… 71

和张仆射塞下曲 (之三) ···························· 72

Reply to Zhang Puye's Border Song (*No. 3*) ········· 73

同李益伤秋 ····································· 74

Share the Sentiments in Fall with Li Yi ············ 75

李 益 Li Yi (748—829?)

江南曲 ··· 76

South of the Yangtze River Song ················ 77

夜上受降城闻笛 ································· 78

Li Yi Mounted the High Wall of the Town

Named Accepting Surrenders

and Heard a Flute Playing at Night ·············· 79

韩 愈 Han Yu (768—824)

晚 春 ··· 80

Late Spring ··································· 81

刘禹锡 Liu Yuxi (772—842)

乌衣巷 ··· 82

Wuyi Lane ···································· 83

竹枝词 (之六) ··································· 84

Song of the Bamboo Branch (*No. 6*) ············· 85

竹枝词 (之七) ··································· 86

Song of the Bamboo Branch (*No. 7*) ············· 87

白居易 Bai Juyi (772—846)

问刘十九 ··· 88

Asking Liu the Nineteenth ························· 89

李 绅 Li Shen (772—846)

悯农 (之一) ··· 90

On the Hardships of Farmers (*No. 1*) ········· 91

悯农 (之二) ··· 92

On the Hardships of Farmers (*No. 2*) ········· 93

崔 护 Cui Hu (772—846)

题都城南庄 ··· 94

Poem Written for the South Village of

the Capital ··· 95

柳宗元 Liu Zongyuan (773—819)

江 雪 ·· 96

Snow on the River ·································· 97

元 稹 Yuan Zhen (779—831)

闻乐天授江州司马 ··································· 98

Hearing that Letian Has Been Designated

the Sima of Jiangzhou ························· 99

贾 岛 Jia Dao (779—843)

寻隐者不遇 ·· 100

Looking for the Recluse but Not Finding Him ·············· 101

杜秋娘 Du Qiuniang (791?—?)

金缕衣 ··· 102

Suit Woven of Gold Thread ······························· 103

杜 牧 Du Mu (803—852)

过华清宫绝句 (之一) ··· 104

Jueju – a Four-line Poem with Seven Words to a Line:

　　Huaqing Palace (No. 1) ······························· 105

赤 壁 ··· 107

Chibi ··· 108

山 行 ··· 110

Trip to the Mountains ···································· 111

泊秦淮 ··· 112

Anchored in the Qinhuai River ························· 113

江南春绝句 ·· 114

Jueju – a Four-line Poem with Seven Words to a Line:

　　Spring South of the Yangtze River ················· 115

秋 夕 ··· 116

Evening on the Seventh Day of the Seventh

　　Month in the Lunar Calendar ······················· 117

赵 嘏 Zhao Gu (806?—853?)

江楼感旧 ·· 119

Memories in the Riverside Building ···················· 120

李商隐 Li Shangyin (813?—858?)

贾　生 ·· 121

The Scholar Jia ·· 122

夜雨寄北 ·· 123

Writing a Letter to the North on a Rainy Night ········· 124

霜　月 ·· 125

Moon in Late Autumn When There Is Frost ············ 126

乐游原 ·· 128

An Overlook for Sightseeing ······························· 129

曹　邺 Cao Ye (816—?)

官仓鼠 ·· 130

Mice in the State Granaries ································· 131

黄　巢 Huang Chao (820—884)

题菊花 ·· 132

On Chrysanthemums ·· 133

菊　花 ·· 134

Chrysanthemum ··· 135

罗　隐 Luo Yin (833—909)

雪 ·· 136

Snow ·· 137

韦　庄 Wei Zhuang (836?—910)

台　城 ·· 138

Taicheng ··· 139

金陵图 ·· 140

A Painting of Jinling City ····························· 141

聂夷中 Nie Yizhong (837—884?)

田　家 ·· 142

Peasant Family ·· 143

杜荀鹤 Du Xunhe (846?—907?)

再经胡城县 ·· 144

Passing through Hucheng County Again ················· 145

韩　翃 Han Hong (?—?)

寒　食 ·· 146

Cold Food Day ·· 147

陈　陶 Chen Tao (?—?)

陇西行 (之二) ·· 149

Trip to Longxi (*No. 2*) ································ 150

金昌绪 Jin Changxu (?—?)

春　怨 ··· 151

Frustration in Spring ································· 152

宋朝诗选
The Song Dynasty Poems
960—1279

王禹偁 Wang Yucheng (954—1001)

畲田词 ··· 154

Burning the Fields in Spring ······················ 155

寇　准 Kou Zhun (961—1023)

书河上亭壁 ·· 156

Writing on the Wall of the River Kiosk ············ 157

范仲淹 Fan Zhongyan (989—1052)

江上渔者 ·· 158

Fisherman on the River ···························· 159

梅尧臣 Mei Yaochen (1002—1060)

陶 者 ··· 160

The Potter ································· 161

欧阳修 Ouyang Xiu (1007—1072)

画眉鸟 ······································· 162

The Thrush ································ 163

苏舜钦 Su Shunqin (1008—1048)

淮中晚泊犊头 ······························· 164

Anchored at Dutou on the Huaihe River at Sunset ··········· 165

王安石 Wang Anshi (1021—1086)

泊船瓜洲 ····································· 167

Anchor at Guazhou ························· 168

梅 花 ······································· 170

Plum Blossoms ···························· 171

书湖阴先生壁 (之一) ······················· 172

Written on the Wall of Master Hu Yin's House (*No. 1*) ········ 173

苏 轼 Su Shi (1037—1101)

题西林壁 ····································· 174

Written on the Wall of Xilin Temple ················ 175

惠崇春江晚景 (之一) ·· 176

A View of the Sunset on the River in Spring

   as Painted by Hui Chong (No. 1) ···················· 177

赠刘景文 ·· 178

For Liu Jingwen ·· 179

饮湖上初晴后雨 (之二) ····································· 181

It Let up and Then Rained Again

   while I Was Drinking on the Lake (No. 2) ··········· 182

黄庭坚 Huang Tingjian (1045—1105)

雨中登岳阳楼望君山 ····································· 183

Looking at Junshan Mountain

   while Climbing Yueyang Tower in the Rain ········ 184

秦 观 Qin Guan (1049—1100)

泗州东城晚望 ·· 186

Looking out in the Evening

   from the Eastern City Wall of Sizhou ·············· 187

陈师道 Chen Shidao (1053—1102)

十七日观潮 ··· 188

Watching the Tide on the Seventeenth Day

   of the Eighth Month in the Lunar Calendar ········ 189

李 纲 Li Gang (1083—1140)

病 牛 ·· 191

The Sick Ox ·· 192

李清照 Li Qingzhao (1084—1151?)

夏日绝句 ·· 193

Jueju — a Four-line Poem with Five Words

to a Line: Summer ·· 194

陆 游 Lu You (1125—1210)

秋夜将晓出篱门迎凉有感 ·································· 195

Early in the Dawn after an Autumn Night

I Walked beyond the Wattle Gate

and Felt the Cold Air and Had Some Thoughts ··········· 196

追感往事 ·· 197

Thoughts from Memories ···································· 198

示 儿 ·· 200

To My Sons ·· 201

十一月四日风雨大作 (之二) ································ 202

During a Big Rainstorm on the Fourth Day

of the Eleventh Month in the Lunar Calendar (*No. 2*) ······ 203

梅花绝句 (之二) ·· 204

Jueju — a Four-line Poem with Seven Words to a Line:

Plum Blossoms (*No. 2*) ··································· 205

范成大 Fan Chengda (1126—1193)

横　塘 ·· 206

Hengtang ·· 207

杨万里 Yang Wangli (1127—1206)

寒　雀 ·· 209

Sparrows in Winter ································ 210

悯　农 ·· 211

Feeling Sad for the Farmers ················ 212

闲居初夏午睡起二绝句 (之一) ············· 213

Jueju — a Four-line Poem with Seven Words to a Line:
Written after Waking up from a Nap during My Early
Summer Vacation (One of the Two) ········· 214

道旁店 ·· 215

An Inn at the Roadside ························ 216

朱　熹 Zhu Xi (1130—1200)

观书有感 ·· 217

A Thought as I Read a Book ················ 218

谢枋得 Xie Fangde (1226—1289)

蚕妇吟 ·· 219

Song from the Woman Who Raises Silkworms ··········· 220

张 愈 Zhang Yu (?—?)

蚕 妇 ·· 221

A Woman Who Raises Silkworms ··················· 222

林 升 Lin Sheng (?—?)

题临安邸 ·· 223

Written on the Wall of the Lin' an Hotel ·············· 224

叶绍翁 Ye Shaoweng (?—?)

游园不值 ·· 225

Visiting a Secluded Garden and Learning

that the Owner Is Away ························· 226

翁 卷 Weng Juan (?—?)

乡村四月 ·· 227

April in the Country ····························· 228

宋朝词选

The Song Dynasty Lyrics for Traditional Melodies
960—1279

柳 永 Liu Yong (987?—1053?)

蝶恋花 ·· 230

Lines for the Dielianhua Melody ················· 231

范仲淹 Fan Zhongyan (989—1052)

渔家傲·秋思 ································· 233

Lines for the Yujiaao Melody: Thoughts of Fall ··········· 234

苏幕遮 ································· 236

Lines for the Sumuzhe Melody ················· 238

晏 殊 Yan Shu (991—1055)

踏莎行 ································· 240

Lines for the Tasuoxing Melody ··········· 241

浣溪沙 ································· 243

Lines for the Huanxisha Melody ··········· 244

采桑子 ································· 246

Lines for the Caisangzi Melody ··········· 247

蝶恋花 ································· 248

Lines for the Dielianhua Melody ··········· 249

欧阳修 Ouyang Xiu (1007—1072)

蝶恋花 ································· 251

Lines for the Dielianhua Melody ··········· 252

玉楼春 ································· 254

Lines for the Yulouchun Melody ·········· 255

苏 轼 Su Shi（1037—1101）

念奴娇·赤壁怀古 ·········· 257

Lines for the Niannujiao Melody:

Recalling Old Times at Chibi ·········· 259

水调歌头 ·········· 262

Lines for the Shuidiaogetou Melody ·········· 264

晏几道 Yan Jidao（1038—1110）

少年游 ·········· 266

Lines for the Shaonianyou Melody ·········· 267

秦 观 Qin Guan（1049—1100）

鹊桥仙 ·········· 269

Lines for the Queqiaoxian Melody ·········· 270

李清照 Li Qingzhao（1084—1155）

如梦令 ·········· 272

Lines for the Rumengling Melody ·········· 273

岳 飞 Yue Fei（1103—1142）

满江红 ·········· 274

Lines for the Manjianghong Melody ················· 276

陆 游 Lu You (1125—1210)

钗头凤 ·· 278

Lines for the Chaitoufeng Melody ················· 280

卜算子·咏梅 ··· 282

Lines for the Busuanzi Melody:

    an Ode to Plum Blossoms ················· 283

夜游宫·记梦寄师伯浑 ························· 285

Lines for the Yeyougong Melody:

    Writing about a Dream

    and Sending the Note to Shi Bohun ·············· 286

辛弃疾 Xin Qiji (1140—1207)

菩萨蛮·书江西造口壁 ························· 288

Lines for the Pusaman Melody:

    Written on the Cliffs at Zaokou in Jiangxi Province ········· 289

青玉案·元夕 ··· 291

Lines for the Qingyu'an Melody:

    the Lantern Festival ·························· 292

鹧鸪天 ·· 294

Lines for the Zhegutian Melody ················· 295

后记——论中国古诗词英译 ································· 297

Epilogue — On the Translation of chinese Classical

    Poems into English ································· 307

唐 朝 诗 选

The Tang Dynasty Poems

618—907

回乡偶书

贺知章

少小离家老大回，

乡音未改鬓毛衰。

儿童相见不相识，

笑问客从何处来。

A Few Lines after Returning to My Hometown

He Zhizhang

left home a child and came back an old old man

my hair has turned gray but my accent is the same

kids in the village did not know me when we met

said where did the guest come from with the funny smile

桃花溪

张　旭

隐隐飞桥隔野烟，

石矶西畔问渔船。

桃花尽日随流水，

洞在青溪何处边。

Mountain River with Peach Blossoms

Zhang Xu

the bridge seems to hover over the river
smoke rises from the meadow behind it

on the west side of a rock
I see a fishing boat and ask

those floating peach blossoms
drift on the river all day long

they must have come from that cave
which side of the river is it on

Mountain River with Peach Blossoms (Taohuaxi) runs at the foot of Taoyuan Mountain in Taoyuan County, Hu'nan Province. **Cave** here may reflect the story written by Tao Yuanming (365?–427), a poet born in Jiujiang City, Jiangxi Province, in the Eastern Jin Dynasty (317–420), titled *A Cave Deep in the Woods of Blooming Peach Trees* , in which a fisherman in Wuling found a sunny world with friendly people inside a cave, who lived a happy life there. After the fisherman returned no one ever could find the cave again.

凉州词

王　翰

葡萄美酒夜光杯，

欲饮琵琶马上催。

醉卧沙场君莫笑，

古来征战几人回。

Liangzhou Song

Wang Han

enticed by the rare grape wine

the polished cup is luminous in darkness

I would drink and drink again

but the thrummed strings of the pipa

urge me again to horse and to war

do not mock me if I stretch out drunk

on that battlefield where no life remains

how many ever survived to come home

since the old days in whatever the war

Liangzhou is in Wuwei City today, Gansu Province. The pipa has been used for over 2000 years. It is shaped like a pear cut half from head to the end. People play it with fingers pulling the four strings. It functions like a guitar.

登鹳雀楼

王之涣

白日依山尽，

黄河入海流。

欲穷千里目，

更上一层楼。

Climbing the Stork Kiosk

Wang Zhihuan

the pale sun is sinking behind the mountain

and the yellow river is running toward the sea

since I want to look at the end of the earth

which is hundreds of miles away

I have to climb these steps to do that

Stork Kiosk （Guanque Tower）stands on the east bank of the Yellow River at Yongji City, Shanxi Province.

凉州词

王之涣

黄河远上白云间，

一片孤城万仞山。

羌笛何须怨杨柳，

春风不度玉门关。

Liangzhou Song

Wang Zhihuan

the Yellow River rises in the tall white clouds

a town is isolated here

it is locked in mountains thousands of feet high

no need for the qiang flute

playing poplar and willow so sad a song

the spring wind never comes to this place

it never warms the other side of Yumen Pass

Liangzhou is in Wuwei City today, Gansu Province. The qiang flute is the bamboo flute with double tubes played by Qiang ethnic minority group who live in the northern part of Sichuan Province. Yumen Pass is in Dunhuang City, Gansu Province.

春　晓

孟浩然

春眠不觉晓，

处处闻啼鸟。

夜来风雨声，

花落知多少。

At Dawn in Spring

Meng Haoran

slept so well I didn't know it was dawn

birds singing in every courtyard woke me up

the wind and rain came to my dream last night

I think of all those petals swept to the ground

宿建德江

孟浩然

移舟泊烟渚，

日暮客愁新。

野旷天低树，

江清月近人。

Anchored at Night on the River in Jiande City

Meng Haoran

my boat lies at anchor

beside an island hidden in mist

it is sundown and I feel even more

the homesickness of the traveller

this is so vast a place

even the nearest trees seem taller

than the skies on the horizon

now the moon sails in clear water

it seems so near

I could almost touch it

River in Jiande City is in Zhejiang Province. It is part of the Xin'an River running through Jiande City.

从军行

王昌龄

青海长云暗雪山，

孤城遥望玉门关。

黄沙百战穿金甲，

不斩楼兰终不还。

Border Duty

Wang Changling

Qinghai clouds shadow the snow-capped mountains
Yumen Pass is a long way to the west

and the border town is isolated
between Qinghai and Yumen

this soldier has fought many times
has defended his barren sandy land

he has met the horsemen in his armour
and his worn-out armour

if I cannot cut down the king of Loulan
he says I will never go home

Qinghai is now Qinghai Province. **Yumen Pass** is in Dunhuag City, Gansu Province. **Loulan** was the name of an ancient city, resided by the Huns. The country Loulan was also named after the city. Loulan vanished centuries ago and its site is now in Xinjiang Uygur Autonomous Region.

出　塞

王昌龄

秦时明月汉时关，

万里长征人未还。

但使龙城飞将在，

不教胡马度阴山。

Beyond the Border

Wang Changling

the brilliant moon and the pass speak to me
of battles we fought in Qin and Han Dynasties

our men hound the invaders
they haven't come home yet

if that high-stepping general
attacking Dragon City were still living

he would command our troops
and no Hu horsemen would cross Yinshan

The general who attacked Dragon City trying to take it back was Li Guang in the Han Dynasty. Dragon City is in Long County today, Hebei Province. Hu horsemen indicates the Huns who invaded China. Yinshan is Yinshan Mountain, in the central part of Inner Mongolia Autonomous Region.

闺 怨

王昌龄

闺中少妇不知愁，

春日凝妆上翠楼。

忽见陌头杨柳色，

悔教夫婿觅封侯。

Bride's Complaint

Wang Changling

she feels happy in her room this morning
puts on her make-up and climbs up the mansion

suddenly she sees below her in the garden
poplar and willow in fresh new colors

thinks bitterly how could she have let him go off
looking for a post as a high court official

九月九日忆山东兄弟

王　维

独在异乡为异客，

每逢佳节倍思亲。

遥知兄弟登高处，

遍插茱萸少一人。

The Ninth Day of the Ninth Month in the Lunar Calendar
I Think of My Brothers on the East Side of the Mountain

Wang Wei

lonesome as an unexpected guest

in a strange village

I miss my family twice over

whenever we celebrate the good festivals

so far from home I picture

the hills where my brothers ramble

and the sweet-scented cornel

tucked in everyone's hair but my own

The ninth day of the ninth month in the lunar calendar is Chongyang Festival, in which people have all kinds of activities to celebrate and enjoy the fall season, one of which is to hike to a higher spot for sightseeing and to tuck cornel into each other's hair or on clothes.

渭城曲

王　维

渭城朝雨浥轻尘，

客舍青青柳色新。

劝君更尽一杯酒，

西出阳关无故人。

Wei City Song

Wang Wei

a dawn rain comes

and settles the dust in Wei City

hotels are soaked deep in dark wet colors

but the willows are a brighter green

why not one more drink for the road

although we have had a few already

once you go west of Yang Pass

old friends are hard to come by

Wei City is today in the northwest of Xi'an City, Shaanxi Province. **Yang Pass** is in Dunhuang City, Gansu Province.

静夜思

李　白

床前明月光，

疑是地上霜。

举头望明月，

低头思故乡。

Thoughts on a Quiet Evening

Li Bai

the floor is flooded with moonlight

frost covers the earth like that

I gaze at the moon from bed

shimmering in a dark hour

sad and homesick

I bow down my head

秋浦歌 (之十四)

李 白

炉火照天地，

红星乱紫烟。

赧郎明月夜，

歌曲动寒川。

Qiupu Song (*No. 14*)

Li Bai

fire booms in the forge

lights up the wide universe

hammer blows shower of sparks

that vanish in purple smoke

the red face of the smith

the white face of the moon

the song of the smith shatters
the dark cold down the valley

Qiupu is in Chizhou City today, Anhui Province.

陪侍郎叔游洞庭醉后

李　白

划却君山好，

平铺湘水流。

巴陵无限酒，

醉杀洞庭秋。

Li Bai Accompanied His Uncle on a Visit to Dongting Lake and Wrote this Poem after Getting Drunk

Li Bai

boat floating around Junshan Mountain
I will flatten this mountain

make the scenery better
water from the Xiangjiang River will run easily

boat comes to Baling town
a good place to drink a lot of wine

we were three sheets to the wind
that fall day on Dongting Lake

Dongting Lake is in the northern part of Hu'nan Province, running into Yangtze River (Changjiang River) at Yueyang. **Junshan Mountain** is in Dongting Lake. Its original name was Dongting Mountain. The lake was named after the mountain. **The Xiangjiang River** runs into Dongting Lake in Hu'nan Province. **Baling** is in Yueyang City today.

峨眉山月歌

李　白

峨眉山月半轮秋，

影入平羌江水流。

夜发清溪向三峡，

思君不见下渝州。

Song of the Moon on Mount Emei

Li Bai

autumn and a half moon on Mount Emei

shadow of the moon dipped into the current

flowing in the Pingqiang River

I left the port of Qingxi this night

and set out for the Three Gorges of the Yangtze River

I long for someone I care for

but I cannot meet with my good friend

sailing by Yuzhou in the quick night

Mount Emei is in Leshan City, Sichuan Province. The Pingqiang River is in Leshan City, Sichuan Province. Qingxi is close to Mount Emei in Sichuan Province. the Three Gorges of the Yangtze River (Changjiang River) are between Baidi in Fengjie County, Chongqing Municipality and Yichang City, Hubei Province. Yuzhou is in Chongqing Municipality today.

望庐山瀑布

李 白

日照香炉生紫烟，

遥看瀑布挂前川。

飞流直下三千尺，

疑是银河落九天。

Watching the Lushan Mountain Falls

Li Bai

purple smoke rises from the mountaintop

the peak of Incense Burner in the sunlight

far away I see the valley stretching before me

the whole waterfall hangs there

the torrent plunges three thousand feet

straight down to the valley floor

I think it must be the Milky Way

spilling to the earth from the heavens

Lushan Mountain is in Jiujiang City, Jiangxi Province.

望天门山

李 白

天门中断楚江开，

碧水东流至此回。

两岸青山相对出，

孤帆一片日边来。

View of Tianmenshan Mountain

Li Bai

I can see Tianmenshan Mountain open like a gate

my boat sails through on the Chu River

the green water running east

turns here in a fierce whirl

green ranges of the mountains

rush toward me from both sides

a single sail bends with the wind

where the sun comes up on the water

Tianmenshan Mountain is in Wuhu City, Anhui Province. It is on both sides of the Yangtze River (Changjiang River) but this part of the Yangtze River is called the **Chu River** because this area belonged to the Chu Kingdom in the Warring States Period (475BC–221BC).

赠汪伦

李 白

李白乘舟将欲行，

忽闻岸上踏歌声。

桃花潭水深千尺，

不及汪伦送我情。

To Wang Lun

Li Bai

I am on board
and the boat ready to sail
when suddenly there is a song
and the rhythm of feet
dancing on the shore

the water in Peach Flower Pond
is a thousand fathoms
but it cannot be deeper
than the affection of Wang Lun
who comes to wave me a goodbye

Wang Lun moved to Jing County, Anhui Province after retiring. His residence was just beside the Peach Flower Pond. Li Bai visited Wang Lun each time he came to tour the Peach Flower Pond.

春夜洛城闻笛

李　白

谁家玉笛暗飞声，

散入春风满洛城。

此夜曲中闻折柳，

何人不起故园情。

Lines while Hearing a Flute Playing One Spring Night in Luo City

Li Bai

I don't know whose house it is

the sound of the jade flute comes from

like a secret spirited on the wind

this evening in spring

it enters every home with that song

Breaking the Willow Branches

and we know what pain

remembering the hometown brings

Luo City is in today's Luoyang City, He'nan Province, an ancient capital for thirteen dynasties. *Breaking the Willow Branches* was a song about the custom in ancient China. To break willow branch while parting meant "I'll miss you".

黄鹤楼送孟浩然之广陵

李　白

故人西辞黄鹤楼，

烟花三月下扬州。

孤帆远影碧空尽，

唯见长江天际流。

Seeing Meng Haoran off

Li Bai

my old friend leaves Yellow Crane Tower

he is going to the east

sailing to Guangling in March

while blossoms curl like smoke on the river

how far away the lone sail

fading into the clear blue sky

only the Yangtze River remains

it is flowing at the edge of the world

Meng Haoran was a well-known poet in the Tang Dynasty and a good friend of Li Bai. The Yellow Crane Tower (Huanghe Tower) stands on the southern bank of the Yangtze River (Changjiang River) on the peak of Snake Mountain in Wuchang, Wuhan City, Hubei Province. Guangling is in Yangzhou City today, Jiangsu Province.

早发白帝城

李 白

朝辞白帝彩云间，

千里江陵一日还。

两岸猿声啼不住，

轻舟已过万重山。

Leaving Baidi City in the Early Morning

Li Bai

Baidi City on the mountaintop
was still swathed in red clouds
when my boat sailed from the foothills
early that morning

I reached Jiangling City in the evening
logging hundreds of miles in one day
monkeys were screaming
on both banks of the Yangtze River

they never let up the whole day's travel
while our light boat dashed between
a thousand mountains lining the river

Baidi City is on top of Baidi Mountain in Fengjie County, Chongqing Municipality. Jiangling was in Jingzhou City, Hubei Province.

逢雪宿芙蓉山主人

刘长卿

日暮苍山远，

天寒白屋贫。

柴门闻犬吠，

风雪夜归人。

Taken in for the Night in My Host's House on Lotus Mountain When I Was Caught in the Snow

Liu Changqing

the great dark mountain

seems far away at sundown

this small white cottage

looks poor and miserable

in such cold weather

the dog barks

at the gate of sticks and branches

my host has come home

he has worked long hours

in the wind-driven snow

Lotus Mountain (Furongshan Mountain) is unable to locate as there are at least more than five mountains named Lotus Mountain in China.

江畔独步寻花

杜　甫

黄四娘家花满蹊，

千朵万朵压枝低。

留连戏蝶时时舞，

自在娇莺恰恰啼。

Alone and Looking for Flowers on the River Bank

Du Fu

flowers applaud both sides of the path

in the courtyard of auntie Huang Si

blossoms thick as sunshine

hang from the heavy branches

the butterflies will not abandon any flower

they dance from one to the other

only now and then

the orioles at their golden pleasure

sing freely and so beautifully

tra-la-heigh-ho no worries today

赠花卿

杜 甫

锦城丝管日纷纷，

半入江风半入云。

此曲只应天上有，

人间能得几回闻。

Song for Hua the Mighty General

Du Fu

in Jinguan City the flutes and the strings

you hear them so loud even in the day time

the melody fades in the river wind

and half in the towering clouds above us

it should never be played here

it belongs to the emperor's heaven

we thank you for what is not ours

but we may not hear it again

Jinguan City is in Chengdu City today, Sichuan Province. Hua was Hua Jingding, a well-known general for victories he won in the Tang Dynasty but the music he played was for the emperor only. It was a crime to violate this rule then.

绝 句

杜 甫

两个黄鹂鸣翠柳，

一行白鹭上青天。

窗含西岭千秋雪，

门泊东吴万里船。

Jueju — a Four-line Poem with Seven Words to a Line

Du Fu

two yellow orioles sing in the tender green willow

a line of white herons crosses the blue sky

the open window has framed

the never-melting snow on West Ridges

the ships sailed in from Dongwu in the east

they lie at anchor in my doorway

West Ridges is Xiling Snow Mountain, in Dayi County, Chengdu City, Sichuan Province. **Dongwu** was the Wu Kingdom, one of the Three Kingdoms in Chinese history, existing between 222 and 280, which had the southeast of China under its control. Nanjing was its capital.

绝　句

杜　甫

江碧鸟逾白，

山青花欲燃，

今春看又过，

何日是归年？

Jueju — a Four-line Poem with Five Words to a Line

Du Fu

river green white water birds

mountain green red flowers afire

another spring dying in colors

what year sends me homeward

八阵图

杜 甫

功盖三分国，

名成八阵图。

江流石不转，

遗恨失吞吴。

The Eight Battle Formations

Du Fu

he had the magnificence

that overwhelmed the Three Kingdoms

his eight battle formations

struck everyone with terror and awe

the stones he used are still in place

despite the flooding of many hundred years

we are left with his shame as he watched

his rash lord turn on the Wu allies

Eight Battle Formations were described in the *Records of the Three Kingdoms*, in which Zhuge Liang, the army commander of Shu Kingdom, created the Eight Battle Formations using lots of stones and won great victories. **Wu** means the Wu Kingdom, one of the Three Kingdoms existing between 222 and 280.

江南逢李龟年

杜 甫

岐王宅里寻常见，

崔九堂前几度闻。

正是江南好风景，

落花时节又逢君。

Meeting Li Guinian in the South of the Yangtze River

Du Fu

I saw you often in lord Qi's house

I heard your singing several times

at the receptions of Cui the Ninth

this is the best season

in the south of the Yangtze River

the scenery is excellent

but the petals have fallen

it is too late for flowers

and now we see each other again

Li Guinian was an outstanding musician in the Tang Dynasty favoured by the emperor. He travelled in the south of the Yangtze River(Changjiang River) in his late years. Lord Qi was the younger brother of the emperor, named Li Fan. Cui the Ninth was the popular author Cui Di, who was the ninth child in his family and was often invited into emperor's palace.

逢入京使

岑　参

故园东望路漫漫，

双袖龙钟泪不干。

马上相逢无纸笔，

凭君传语报平安。

Meeting the Envoy on His Way to the Capital

Cen Shen

I see that the road is long and endless

when I look back to my hometown in the east

I wipe my eyes on my sleeves

but there are too many tears to dry them

now because we meet on horseback on the highway

there is no place to find a brush pen or paper

so please take this message to my family in the capital

I feel alright and no one has threatened me

枫桥夜泊

张　继

月落乌啼霜满天，

江枫渔火对愁眠。

姑苏城外寒山寺，

夜半钟声到客船。

Anchored at Night near Maple Bridge

Zhang Ji

the old moon is going down
and the crows make a ruckus
the world is covered with frost

there are maples on the riverbank
and the lights of fishing boats
drift with the current

I fall into a sad sleep
the Cold Mountain Temple
it is outside the town of Gusu

the sound of its bell at midnight
touches the guest in this boat

Maple Bridge is in Suzhou City, Jiangsu Province. **The town of Gusu** is Suzhou City today. **The Cold Mountain Temple** (Hanshan Temple) is in Suzhou City, Jiangsu Province, belonging to Zen Buddhism.

滁州西涧

韦应物

独怜幽草涧边生，

上有黄鹂深树鸣。

春潮带雨晚来急，

野渡无人舟自横。

The Western Ravine in Chuzhou

Wei Yingwu

I am fond of the tranquil grass

that grows alongside the ravine

orioles are singing above it

hidden in the huge green trees

spring sends rain to the river

it rushes in a flood in the evening

the little boat tugs at its line

by the ferry landing

here in the wilderness

it responds to the current

there is no one on board

Chuzhou is in Chuzhou City today, Anhui Province.

听　筝

李　端

鸣筝金粟柱，

素手玉房前。

欲得周郎顾，

时时误拂弦。

Listening to Zither Playing

Li Duan

the resonant strings tremble

on the golden pillars of the zither

slender white fingers dance at the frets

there in front of the man general Zhou

she touches a wrong note now and then

coaxing a glance from the general

General Zhou was Zhou Yu (175–120), the commander of the army in the Wu Kingdom, one of the Three Kingdoms existing between 222 and 280 in Chinese history, who knew music very well.

塞上曲

戎 昱

胡风略地烧连山，

碎叶孤城未下关。

山头烽子声声叫，

知是将军夜猎还。

Border Ballad

Rong Yu

the Hu horsemen came raiding

they burned down many places in the mountains

the border town of Suiye

that city's gate was not locked shut

guards on the watch towers

shouted from one to the other

all the way into the city

they knew the general was galloping

back from the night hunt

Suiye is in Kyrgyzstan Republic. The site of the city is beside Tokmok, which is close to Bishkek, the capital of the country. It was a town on the Silk Road.

和张仆射塞下曲（之二）

卢　纶

林暗草惊风，

将军夜引弓。

平明寻白羽，

没在石棱中。

Reply to Zhang Puye's Border Song (*No. 2*)

Lu Lun

it was getting dark and the woods darker

and the uneasy wind

disturbed the meadow

the commander drew his bowstring

taut in the night

we looked for his feathered shaft

when dawn came again

we found it on a rocky slope

driven deep into a crevice on a huge rock

Puye was a title of official at the time. There are no records available for either General Zhang Puye or his poems.

和张仆射塞下曲 (之三)

卢 纶

月黑雁飞高，

单于夜遁逃。

欲将轻骑逐，

大雪满弓刀。

Reply to Zhang Puye's Border Song (*No. 3*)

Lu Lun

dark of the moon

and the wild geese flying high

Chan Yu lost the battle

and fled into the night

our light cavalry

quick mounted and chased him

came back saddle sore and exhausted

sleet freezing on their bows and knives

Chan Yu was the leader of the Huns, who invaded the inner land of China from the northwest but was completely beaten in the Han Dynasty.

同李益伤秋

卢　纶

岁去人头白，

秋来树叶黄。

搔头向黄叶，

与尔共悲伤。

Share the Sentiments in Fall with Li Yi

Lu Lun

so many years today

my hair sparse and white

and this is another autumn

leaves yellow and dry

I scratch my head

and complain to those leaves

the deep sadness

they have fallen to share

Li Yi (748–829?) was born in Guzang, Liangzhou. It is in Wuwei City, Gansu Province today. He was an important poet of the Tang Dynasty, well-known for his border songs.

江南曲

李　益

嫁得瞿塘贾，

朝朝误妾期。

早知潮有信，

嫁与弄潮儿。

South of the Yangtze River Song

Li Yi

I got married to a merchant

who lives beside Qutang Gorge

he goes off in the morning

and works for his money all night long

the tide rises and the tide falls

I should have thought about that

and married myself a good sailor

whose boat goes out and comes in on the tide

Qutang is one of the Three Gorges of the Yangtze River (Changjiang River).

夜上受降城闻笛

李 益

回乐烽前沙似雪，

受降城外月如霜。

不知何处吹芦管，

一夜征人尽望乡。

Li Yi Mounted the High Wall of the Town Named Accepting Surrenders and Heard a Flute Playing at Night

Li Yi

the sand spreads like a snowfield
before the watch tower in Huile County

beyond the town named Accepting Surrenders
the moonlight is a blanket of frost

the soft melody of the flute
where is it coming from

all night the soldiers at their posts
look into the darkness for their homes

Li Yi was an important poet of the Tang Dynasty, well-known for his border songs. The town named Accepting Surrenders is on the Western Hills in Kundulungou of Baotou City, Inner Mongolia Autonomous Region. Huile County is in Lingwu County today, Ningxia Hui Autonomous Region.

晚　春

韩　愈

草树知春不久归，

百般红紫斗芳菲。

杨花榆荚无才思，

惟解漫天作雪飞。

Late Spring

Han Yu

meadows and trees know

that spring will be over soon

they vie with each other

with all the purples and reds

and fragrances of colors

poplars burst in white cotton

the elms follow

whirling white seeds in the air

what wisdom do they have

blowing around us like snow

乌衣巷

刘禹锡

朱雀桥边野草花，

乌衣巷口夕阳斜。

旧时王谢堂前燕，

飞入寻常百姓家。

Wuyi Lane

Liu Yuxi

the weeds are in flower
beside the Zhuque Bridge

the evening sun drops low
at the entrance of Wuyi Lane

aristocrats Wang and Xie
lived there in Jin Dynasty

swallows nested in their houses
now ordinary people live with the birds

Wuyi Lane is in Qinhuai District, Nanjing City, Jiangsu Province.
Zhuque Bridge was one of the 24 floating bridges built across the Qinhuai
River in Nanjing before the Tang Dynasty. **Wang and Xie** refer to the families
of Wang Dao and Xie An , Premiers of the Eastern Jin Dynasty, who lived in
this Wuyi Lane.

竹枝词 (之六)

刘禹锡

城西门前滟滪堆，

年年波浪不能摧。

懊恼人心不如石，

少时东去复西来。

Song of the Bamboo Branch (*No. 6*)

Liu Yuxi

out in front of the town's Western Gate

the great rock stands in the middle of the river

powerful waves bash it year in and year out

but they cannot wash it away

it makes me sad the human heart

doesn't rest as solid as this stone

the heart goes to the east for a while

and then goes west a split second later

Bamboo Branch was originally a folksong in Sichuan Province. Poet Liu Yuxi was the first to start collecting, mimicking, and absorbing its essence in his own poem writing. **The great rock** (Yanyudui) was over 60 metres above the surface of water at the mouth of Qutang Gorge in the middle of the Yangtze River (Changjiang River). It was removed in the middle of the 20th century.

竹枝词（之七）

刘禹锡

瞿塘嘈嘈十二滩，

人言道路古来难。

长恨人心不如水，

等闲平地起波澜。

Song of the Bamboo Branch (*No. 7*)

Liu Yuxi

the Qutang Gorge has twelve rapids

the river rushes the channel

with a long swish and a roar

people have said since the old days

it's a hard way to go whatever you do

what a sorry business this is

how pitiful the human heart is

the rapids make wild waves in the gorges

but the trouble people make is shameful

when things run as smooth as open water

Bamboo Branch was originally a folksong in Sichuan Province. Poet Liu Yuxi was the first to start collecting, mimicking, and absorbing its essence in his own poem writing.

问刘十九

白居易

绿蚁新醅酒，

红泥小火炉，

晚来天欲雪，

能饮一杯无？

Asking Liu the Nineteenth

Bai Juyi

that newly fermented rice wine

still has tiny green particles floating

it is called the green ants wine

and the little red-clay stove is red with fire

it is going to snow

late in the afternoon

shall we get together

and have us a cup of the wine

Liu the Nineteenth was the poet's cousin.

悯农 （之一）

李　绅

春种一粒粟，

秋收万颗子。

四海无闲田，

农夫犹饿死。

On the Hardships of Farmers (*No. 1*)

Li Shen

they sow one seed of millet in spring

and harvest ten thousand in the fall

they do not waste an inch of land anywhere

but they are still dying of famine

悯农 (之二)

李 绅

锄禾日当午，

汗滴禾下土。

谁知盘中餐，

粒粒皆辛苦。

On the Hardships of Farmers (*No. 2*)

Li Shen

when they chop weeds at noon

the sun scorches their heads

they soak the ground underneath the rows

with the trickle of their sweat

count each grain in your dish

it grew from hard work and exhaustion

how many people know this

题都城南庄

崔　护

去年今日此门中，

人面桃花相映红。

人面不知何处去，

桃花依旧笑春风。

Poem Written for the South Village of the Capital

Cui Hu

last year on this morning

I walked through the village

in one courtyard

I saw the face of a woman

and the peach blossoms

a pale red reflecting pale red

now I see the courtyard empty

the woman no longer there

only the peach blossoms

tremble on the wind

The capital was Chang'an.

江 雪

柳宗元

千山鸟飞绝，

万径人踪灭。

孤舟蓑笠翁，

独钓寒江雪。

Snow on the River

Liu Zongyuan

no singing of birds in the mountain ranges

no footprints of men on a thousand trails

there is only one boat on the water

with an old man in a straw rain cape

who sits on the deck and fishes by himself

where the snow falls on the cold river

闻乐天授江州司马

元　稹

残灯无焰影幢幢，

此夕闻君谪九江。

垂死病中惊坐起，

暗风吹雨入寒窗。

Hearing that Letian Has Been Designated the Sima of Jiangzhou

Yuan Zhen

the candle is guttering out

there is very little flame

I see shadows all around me

this evening I hear that my friend

has been demoted to Jiujiang

even though I am sick to dying

I sit up in fear and surprise

this dark night the wind

blows a cold rain

through the cracks in my window

Letian is the other name for the poet Bai Juyi. **Jiangzhou** is Jiujiang today in Jiangxi Province. **Sima** was the Governor's consultant, who had no power at all.

寻隐者不遇

贾　岛

松下问童子，

言师采药去。

只在此山中，

云深不知处。

Looking for the Recluse but Not Finding Him

Jia Dao

I ask the boy under the pine trees

he says my master went off

to pick some medicinal herbs

he is a little way up on this mountain

but the clouds are so thick

I can't tell you where he is

金缕衣

杜秋娘

劝君莫惜金缕衣，

劝君惜取少年时。

花开堪折直须折，

莫待花无空折枝。

Suit Woven of Gold Thread

Du Qiuniang

friend take my advice

don't worry about a gold-threaded suit

listen to me my friend

make the best of your spring days

go for the best of the flowers

when everything is in bloom

don't wait until the blossoms have fallen

what good will a branch do you then

过华清宫绝句(之一)

杜 牧

长安回望绣成堆，

山顶千门次第开。

一骑红尘妃子笑，

无人知是荔枝来。

Jueju — a Four-line Poem with Seven Words to a Line: Huaqing Palace (*No.1*)

Du Mu

looking back again from Chang'an

I see the beautiful palace

it stands like piles of silk

embroidered in the mountains

doors open one after the other

leading to the upper chamber

the plunging horse will soon

gallop into the palace yard

and Yang the concubine is smiling

she is the emperor's favorite

she watches the clouds of the dust

no one else knows the litchi is coming

Huaqing Palace is in Lintong, Xi'an City, Shaanxi Province. Chang'an was the capital of the Tang Dynasty. It is called Xi'an today. Litchi was the favorite fruit of Concubine Yang but litchi was only grown far down in the south of China.

赤 壁

杜 牧

折戟沉沙铁未销，

自将磨洗认前朝。

东风不与周郎便，

铜雀春深锁二乔。

Chibi

Du Mu

the shattered halberd in the sand

is not totally corroded

I wash it and give it a polish

and it tells me of earlier dynasties

how general Zhou in the Wu Kingdom

had a lucky east wind

or else his wife and his lord's wife

the Qiao sisters

would have been caught

by the lord of the Wei Kingdom

he would have made them comfort him

locked in the bronze bird roof tower

Chibi is in the southeast of Hubei Province and on the south of the Yangtze River (Changjiang River). During the Three Kingdoms (220-280) the allied forces of the Wu and Shu Kingdoms crushed the force of the Wei Kingdom by setting fire to the enemy's fleet with the help of the wind from the east. **General Zhou** was Zhou Yu (175-210), the commander of the army of the Wu Kingdom. **Qiao sisters** were from Qianshan, Anhui Province and well-known beautiful women in the Three Kingdoms time. The younger one of the sisters was born in 180 and married Zhou Yu in 196.

山　行

杜　牧

远上寒山石径斜，

白云生处有人家。

停车坐爱枫林晚，

霜叶红于二月花。

Trip to the Mountains

Du Mu

the narrow stone trail

winds far up into the mountains

this is a cloudy place

the cabins are almost invisible

I love seeing the maples at sunset

and pause in my cart to watch them

the leaves are as red

as prairies in the early flowering spring

泊秦淮

杜　牧

烟笼寒水月笼沙，

夜泊秦淮近酒家。

商女不知亡国恨，

隔江犹唱后庭花。

Anchored in the Qinhuai River

Du Mu

fog is shrouding the cold water

moonlight floods the sandy beach

my boat is anchored in the Qinhuai River

a wine shop is handy on the shore

the entertaining girl doesn't weep

for the fall of the dynasty but sings

Flowers in the Rear Garden by the emperor

just on the other side of the river

The Qinhuai River runs through Nanjing City, Jiangsu Province. The emperor was Chen Shubao (553–604), the last emperor (582–589) of the Chen Dynasty, who wrote the lines for the melody of *Jade Tree Flowers in the Rear Garden*, in which this line "Jade tree flowers bloom, but they will not last long" was considered an omen predicting his loss of the empire.

江南春绝句

杜　牧

千里莺啼绿映红，

水村山郭酒旗风。

南朝四百八十寺，

多少楼台烟雨中。

Jueju — a Four-line Poem with Seven Words to a Line: Spring South of the Yangtze River

Du Mu

orioles are singing in a green and red

profusion of color for a thousand miles

in small towns along rivers and hills

the tavern signs are blowing in the wind like flags

they built four hundred and eighty temples

during the time of the Southern Dynasties

those buildings and their terraces

lie half hidden in the mist and the rain

Southern Dynasties existed from 420 to 589 including the Song, Qi, Liang and Chen Kingdoms.

秋 夕

杜 牧

银烛秋光冷画屏，

轻罗小扇扑流萤。

天阶夜色凉如水，

坐看牵牛织女星。

Evening on the Seventh Day of the Seventh Month in the Lunar Calendar

Du Mu

white candles are burning

autumn is in the air

and the room panels are cold

she swipes at fireflies with a little fan

a fan delicate and made of silk

she is sitting by the staircase

at the front of the house

the autumn wind

chilly as a mountain stream

she watches the one star and the other

Altair and Vega

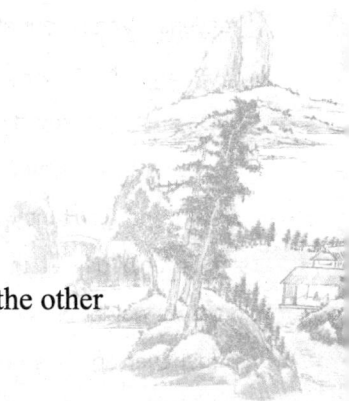

the cowherd and the woman at the loom

from the old legend

The old legend: the cowherd (**Altair**) married the fairy maiden from the heavens (**Vega**), but after giving birth to two children the fairy maiden was taken away by soldiers sent by the King of the heavens. With the help of a piece of skin offered by a cow he flew over to the sky with their two children to chase after her but he couldn't cross over the Silver River (the Milky Way). As a result they were allowed to meet once a year in the evening on the seventh day of the seventh month in the lunar calendar. Since then magpies gather on top of the Silver River to form a bridge with their wings in that evening. This helps the couple, mother and children with their short reunion.

江楼感旧

赵　嘏

独上江楼思渺然，

月光如水水如天。

同来望月人何处？

风景依稀似去年。

Memories in the Riverside Building

Zhao Gu

as I climb alone the steps of the building

my sadness confuses my heart

the moonlight on the water reflects the sky

who can tell the one from the other

those who enjoyed this light with me last year

where can I find them or turn to them now

and yet this still seems to be the same

moon-shadowed world we looked at then

贾 生

李商隐

宣室求贤访逐臣，

贾生才调更无伦。

可怜夜半虚前席，

不问苍生问鬼神。

The Scholar Jia

Li Shangyin

the emperor sought for talented officials
among the exiled ministers of the Han Dynasty
he met with them at his Weiyang Palace

and Jia the scholar came
no one could match his intelligence

the emperor spoke with him until midnight
leaning forward in the lotus position

the emperor wanted to know
all this scholar knew about ghosts and gods

jia could have told him how to save the state
take care of the ordinary people

Scholar Jia was the well-known scholar and reformer Jia Yi (200BC–168BC) who was banished in Han Dynasty. Weiyang Palace was in Chang'an in the Han Dynasty.

夜雨寄北

李商隐

君问归期未有期，

巴山夜雨涨秋池。

何当共剪西窗烛，

却话巴山夜雨时。

Writing a Letter to the North on a Rainy Night

Li Shangyin

you ask me when I will be coming home
but I cannot tell you exactly

tonight the autumn rain on Bashan Mountain
makes the ponds rise to overflowing

when will we be able to sit together
at the window that looks out on the west

just two of us talking there so long
we will have to trim the wicks of our candles

speaking about our lives this night
when it was raining on Bashan Mountain

Bashan Mountain is in the connected border area of Shaanxi Province, Sichuan Province and Hubei Province.

霜 月

李商隐

初闻征雁已无蝉，

百尺楼高水接天。

青女素娥俱耐冷，

月中霜里斗婵娟。

Moon in Late Autumn When There Is Frost

Li Shangyin

as soon as we heard the calling of the geese

heading south in their high formations

we knew that the noise of the cicada was ended

on top of the building a hundred feet up

you can see the water merge with the sky

far in the distance at the edge of things

the goddess of frost and snow deep in the heavens

and Chang'e the woman who went to the moon

neither one of them is afraid of the cold

they cheer each other on to make the world lovely

the one covers the earth with a gleaming blanket

the other suffuses the darkness with her light

Chang'e was a daughter of one of the earliest emperors in Chinese legend, who secretly took the medicine her husband got from the heavens and flew all of a sudden into the moon and was supposed to stay there forever.

乐游原

李商隐

向晚意不适,

驱车登古原。

夕阳无限好,

只是近黄昏。

An Overlook for Sightseeing

Li Shangyin

feeling sorrowful at the day's end

I drive my cart to the ancient overlook

the sun going down is truly beautiful

how sad the night comes so quickly after

The **overlook** (Leyouyuan) is in the southeast of Xi'an City.

官仓鼠

曹 邺

官仓老鼠大如斗，
见人开仓亦不走。
健儿无粮百姓饥，
谁遣朝朝入君口。

Mice in the State Granaries

Cao Ye

mice in the state granaries are as big as buckets

they don't even run when you open the doors

soldiers at the front want food

ordinary people have to go hungry

who gave these big mice permission

to stuff their bellies all day long

题菊花

黄　巢

飒飒西风满院栽，

蕊寒香冷蝶难来。

他年我若为青帝，

报与桃花一处开。

On Chrysanthemums

Huang Chao

they are in color everywhere in the courtyard

leaning against the chill of the west wind

no butterflies hang on the cold stamens

or linger in the pungent fragrance

if in some year I become the god of flowers

I will set them glowing among the peach blossoms

菊 花

黄 巢

待到秋来九月八，

我花开后百花杀。

冲天香阵透长安，

满城尽带黄金甲。

Chrysanthemum

Huang Chao

my chrysanthemums are flowering everywhere

in late autumn by the eighth of September

when five score other plants are withered

their sharp fragrance rises to the heavens

the whole city of Chang'an is filled with it

my golden armour seizes every nook and cranny

Chang'an was the capital of the Tang Dynasty. **The eighth of September** meant in the lunar calendar.

雪

罗　隐

尽道丰年瑞，

丰年事若何。

长安有贫者，

为瑞不宜多。

Snow

Luo Yin

everybody says snow in winter

means a bumper crop next fall

what good did it do the last time

we had so much snow

there are many poor people

living in Chang'an City

we may need snow for a good harvest

but spare them the cruel blizzards

Chang'an was the capital of the Tang Dynasty.

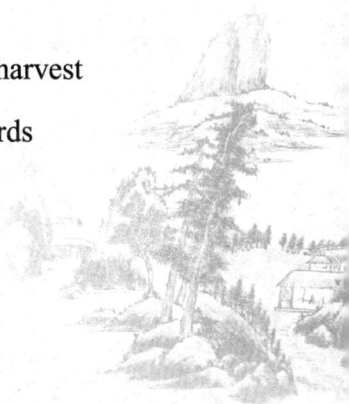

台 城

韦 庄

江雨霏霏江草齐，

六朝如梦鸟空啼。

无情最是台城柳，

依旧烟笼十里堤。

Taicheng

Wei Zhuang

heavy rains along the river

the grass on the banks is flourishing

Six Dynasties rose and fell here like a dream

now it is just the birds and their empty songs

willows drift in the winds of Taicheng

like clouds of undulant smoke

they cover the ten mile levee

as imperturbable as ever

Taicheng is beside Xuanwu Lake in Nanjing City, Jiangsu Province. The Six Dynasties (222–589) include the Wu, Eastern Jin, South Song, South Qi, South Liang and South Chen dynasties (listed by sequence). Nanjing was the capital for all the Six Dynasties.

金陵图

韦　庄

谁谓伤心画不成。

画人心逐世人情。

君看六幅南朝事，

老木寒云满故城。

A Painting of Jinling City

Wei Zhuang

who says a painter cannot reflect

sorrows in his painting

the painter ignores the reality

and panders to common people

but observe these six paintings

that reflect the Southern Dynasties

gnarled trees and cold clouds

see how they shadow the ancient city

Jinling City is Nanjing today in Jiangsu Province, the capital of the Six Dynasties in the south of the Yangtze River(Changjiang River). They fell one after another.

田 家

聂夷中

父耕原上田，

子劚山下荒。

六月禾未秀，

官家已修仓！

Peasant Family

Nie Yizhong

father cultivates the fields on the valley floor

his son tends the land at the foot of the mountain

their crops have not flowered yet in June

the state begins repairing the granaries

再经胡城县

杜荀鹤

去岁曾经此县城，

县民无口不冤声。

今来县宰加朱绂，

便是生灵血染成。

Passing through Hucheng County Again

Du Xunhe

I stopped at this county last year

and everybody was complaining

now this year I see

the administrator wearing a new red stole

he has smeared his badge of office

with the blood of the common people

Hucheng County in now Fuyang County, Anhui Province.

寒 食

韩 翃

春城无处不飞花，

寒食东风御柳斜。

日暮汉宫传蜡烛，

轻烟散入五侯家。

Cold Food Day

Han Hong

blossoms were falling everywhere

in the city that spring

and the east wind rustled the willow

in the emperor's garden

on the Cold Food Day

at sundown that day in the Han Dynasty

burning candles were handed out

and these were reserved

for the five noble eunuchs

honoured with the title of Hou

who incensed their courtyards

with the gray willow smoke

Cold Food Day is the day before Qingming Festival in spring. It is a day for having only cold meals to avoid using fire in memory of a hero, Jie Zitui, who was burnt to death when the emperor ordered the mountain set on fire hoping to get this well-known hermit out to honour him because the hermit once saved the emperor's life. **Qingming Festival** is known for worshipping at the ancestral graves and sweeping graves clean. **Title Hou** was a title lower only than Lord at that time.

陇西行 (之二)

陈　陶

誓扫匈奴不顾身，

五千貂锦丧胡尘。

可怜无定河边骨，

犹是春闺梦里人。

Trip to Longxi (*No. 2*)

Chen Tao

they swore to wipe out the Hu invaders
they didn't care about their own safety

five thousand lances were broken
when the Hu horsemen struck them

it is so pitiful seeing the white bones
scattered along the Wuding River

these relics are the husbands
their wives are still waiting in dreams

Trip to Longxi was an old title for a melody in ancient China, which was collected into Yuefu, the name of a government agency in charge of collecting folk songs and folk music since the Qin Dynasty. Longxi is the west side of Long Mountain in Dingxi City, Gansu Province. The Wuding River is a branch of the Yellow River in Yulin City, Shaanxi Province. Hu here indicates the Huns as a minority in the west invading the inner land in the Han Dynasty.

春 怨

金昌绪

打起黄莺儿，

莫教枝上啼。

啼时惊妾梦，

不得到辽西。

Frustration in Spring

Jin Changxu

get rid of those songbirds

they are noisy in the trees

they spoiled my sweet dream

I couldn't meet my husband in Liaoxi

Liaoxi is today in the west of the Liaohe River in Liaoning Province and north of Shanhai Pass in Hebei Province.

宋 朝 诗 选

The Song Dynasty Poems

960—1279

畲田词

王禹偁

北山种了种南山，

相助刀耕岂有偏。

愿得人间皆似我，

也应四海少荒田。

Burning the Fields in Spring

Wang Yucheng

we plant those slopes

on north mountain

and after that do the fields

on south mountain

everyone helps with spring plowing

each one does a fair share

everybody in the world

should be like us

and less land would be wasted

anywhere in the world

书河上亭壁

寇　准

岸阔樯稀波渺茫，

独凭危槛思何长。

萧萧远树疏林外，

一半秋山带夕阳。

Writing on the Wall of the River Kiosk

Kou Zhun

there is a scattering
of tall masts along the shore
creation absorbs the river
beyond the horizon

atop the tower
I lean against the guardrail
and sense the fear of a height
my thoughts deep and eternal

the leaves are falling
from one or two trees
I can see them far away there
at the edge of the forest

half the autumn mountain in shadow
darkness is leading the sun down

江上渔者

范仲淹

江上往来人，

但爱鲈鱼美。

君看一叶舟，

出没风波里。

Fisherman on the River

Fan Zhongyan

people by the river

cross over and back

they love the beauty of the perch

and the taste of it

but have you seen the small boat

like a curling leaf

sail out and return

on the waves and the wind

陶　者

梅尧臣

陶尽门前土，

屋上无片瓦。

十指不沾泥，

鳞鳞居大厦。

The Potter

Mei Yaochen

the potter in front of his door
uses up all the clay
he doesn't have one tile left over
for the roof of his house

those who never mould clay
with their own ten fingers
have gables on fine halls
tiled like fish scales

画眉鸟

欧阳修

百啭千声随意移，

山花红紫树高低。

始知锁向金笼听，

不及林间自在啼。

The Thrush

Ouyang Xiu

a hundred small whistles

a thousand sweet tunes

whenever this bird wants to warble

it flies to the red and purple streaked flowers

or anywhere in the crowns of trees

this thrush knows about freedom

better singing in the woods

than thrilling in a gold-plated bamboo cage

oh the forest hour after hour

all this pleasure for a song

淮中晚泊犊头

苏舜钦

春阴垂野草青青，

时有幽花一树明。

晚泊孤舟古祠下，

满川风雨看潮生。

Anchored at Dutou
on the Huaihe River at Sunset

Su Shunqin

spring clouds adrift

above the vast land

their shadows wander

the dark greens of the meadows

here and there a branch in blossom

small bright greetings

in the sheltering leaves

my solitary boat

anchored at sundown

by an ancient ancestral temple

close to the shore

I watch the tide

slipping in so quietly

and the ruffle of the wind and rain

on the river

Dutou is a small town in Huaiyin County, Jiangsu Province. The Huaihe River runs through He'nan, Anhui and Jiangsu provinces between the Yellow River and the Yangtze River (Changjiang River).

泊船瓜洲

王安石

京口瓜洲一水间，

钟山只隔数重山。

春风又绿江南岸，

明月何时照我还？

Anchor at Guazhou

Wang Anshi

Jingkou and Guazhou

the distance which separates them

is only at about as far

as the width of the Yangtze River

Zhongshan Mountain

how it looms there

almost on top of me

with only a few ranges in between

spring winds are blowing

south of the river

and everything

everything is green again

when will the year come

that I can go home

with the bright moon

my companion on the road

Guazhou is in Yangzhou City, Jiangsu Province, which sits on the northern shore of the Yangtze. Jingkou is in Zhenjiang City in Jiangsu Province, which sits on the southern shore of the Yangtze. Zhongshan Mountain is Zijin Mountain in Nanjing City where the poet's family resided.

梅 花

王安石

墙角数枝梅，

凌寒独自开。

遥知不是雪，

为有暗香来。

Plum Blossoms

Wang Anshi

a lonesome corner

just a few

branches with plum blossoms

so white

stretch against the cold

the wind

carries such fragrance

you can tell

it is not snowing

where the plums stand

书湖阴先生壁 (之一)

王安石

茅檐长扫静无苔，

花木成畦手自栽。

一水护田将绿绕，

两山排闼送青来。

Written on the Wall of Master Hu Yin's House (No. 1)

Wang Anshi

you clean under the thatched roofs frequently

there is no moss growing in them

lines of trees and straight flower beds

you have planted them and raised them yourself

a river protects your land

it circles the lush fields

open the gate in your yard

and look there are two green hills

Hu Yin was neighbour of the poet when the poet lived in Nanjing after he retired. Hu Yin's formal name was Yang Defeng.

题西林壁

苏 轼

横看成岭侧成峰，

远近高低各不同。

不识庐山真面目，

只缘身在此山中。

Written on the Wall of Xilin Temple

Su Shi

behold this world horizontally
and it appears all ranges
or stare at it vertically
and peaks scrape the clouds

high or low
far or near
all this individuality
teaming in diversity

how can we recognize
the real face of Lushan Mountain
we who wonder here
so deep in the mountains

Xilin Temple was built in the year 366 on the northern side of Lushan Mountain in Jiangxi Province.

惠崇春江晚景(之一)

苏　轼

竹外桃花三两枝，

春江水暖鸭先知。

蒌蒿满地芦芽短，

正是河豚欲上时。

A View of the Sunset on the River in Spring as Painted by Hui Chong (*No. 1*)

Su Shi

a few branches of peach blossoms

extend above the bamboo grove

ducks are the first to know

when the river warms in spring

wormwood grows everywhere

around the young asparagus shoots

this is the time of year the globe fish

gleam beneath the sunlight on the water

Hui Chong was a monk (965–1017), born in Jianyang, Fujian Province. He was a very famous painter in the Song Dynasty.

赠刘景文

苏 轼

荷尽已无擎雨盖，

菊残犹有傲霜枝。

一年好景君须记，

最是橙黄橘绿时。

For Liu Jingwen

Su Shi

the poor lotus petals
discolor and wither now
where are the big leaves
that sheltered them

the hearty chrysanthemums
are beginning to droop
although all of their stems
still brave the frost

old friend we must keep in mind
the year at its best

with its golden oranges

and tangerines like jade

Liu Jingwen was a good friend of Su Shi. He was from Kaifeng of He'
nan Province and a poet in the Song Dynasty （1033-1092）. He once
worked as a deputy commander of Zhejiang Province and met Su Shi in
Hangzhou.

饮湖上初晴后雨(之二)

苏 轼

水光潋滟晴方好，

山色空蒙雨亦奇。

欲把西湖比西子，

淡妆浓抹总相宜。

It Let up and Then Rained Again
while I Was Drinking on the Lake (No. 2)

Su Shi

the light sparkling on the waves
looks very fine when the weather is good

and how mysterious it seems when it rains
and the hills are veiled in mist

I like to think of the beautiful Xishi
and compare this West Lake to her

she can use heavy make-up or light
either way the man who sees her is happy

Xishi was one of the four most beautiful women in ancient China. Her name was Shi Yiguang and she was born in today's Zhuji City, Zhejiang Province. She was born in the Yue Kingdom the late years of the Spring and Autumn Period (770BC–476BC). There are no records about the year of her birth.

雨中登岳阳楼望君山

黄庭坚

投荒万死鬓毛斑，

生出瞿塘滟滪关。

未到江南先一笑，

岳阳楼上对君山。

满川风雨独凭栏，

绾结湘娥十二鬟。

可惜不当湖水面，

银山堆里看青山。

Looking at Junshan Mountain
while Climbing Yueyang Tower in the Rain

Huang Tingjian

I have known so many dangers in this exile

my sideburns are beginning to turn gray

now I have survived

the Qutang Gorge and Yanyu Rock

suddenly I break into laughter

before I come south of the Yangtze

now I look at Junshan Mountain

from the top of Yueyang Tower

I stand against the rail alone

while the wind fills the valley with rain

like the goddess of the Xiangjiang River

she has wound her hair in twelve coils

oh I wish I could go down

where the surf is rolling on the lake

and see that towering green mountain

beyond the white ranges of the waves

The Qutang Gorge is one of the Three Gorges of the Yangtze River (Changjiang River). **Yanyu Rock** (Yanyudui) was over 60 metres above the surface of water at the mouth of the Qutang Gorge in the middle of the Yangtze River. It was removed in the middle of 20th century. **Junshan Mountain** is in Dongting Lake. Its original name was Dongting Mountain. The lake was named after the mountain.

泗州东城晚望

秦 观

渺渺孤城白水环，

舳舻人语夕霏间。

林梢一抹青如画，

应是淮流转处山。

Looking out in the Evening from the Eastern City Wall of Sizhou

Qin Guan

the white water looks so far away
it is almost invisible

the river is a band circling the lone town
and sunset clouds fill with ships and voices

beyond this scene the forest looks like
a green stroke painted on the sky

that should be the moutain
where the Huaihe River makes a turn

Sizhou is in Xuyi County, Jiangsu Province. It was completely buried under mud and sand due to the Yellow River flood in 1680. The Huaihe River runs through He'nan, Anhui and Jiangsu provinces between the Yellow River and the Yangtze River (Changjiang River).

十七日观潮

陈师道

漫漫平沙走白虹，

瑶台失手玉杯空。

晴天摇动清江底，

晚日浮沉急浪中。

Watching the Tide on the Seventeenth Day of the Eighth Month in the Lunar Calendar

Chen Shidao

waves like alabaster rainbows

walk up the vast sandy beach

and the jade cup

dropped from the penthouse

of the gods

emptying all the water down

the opaque sky

shifts violently

on the bottom of the clear river

the sun on its evening journey

bobs in the waves

rising and falling

on the rushing waters

Watching the tide indicates watching the tide at the mouth of the Qiantang River in Zhejiang Province where the rising tide from the sea rushes into the river, pushing the river current back to create huge waves. The sixteenth day to the eighteenth day of the eighth month in the lunar calendar has been known the best time of the year to watch the tide.

病 牛

李 纲

耕犁千亩实千箱，

力尽筋疲谁复伤。

但得众生皆得饱，

不辞羸病卧残阳。

The Sick Ox

Li Gang

opened a thousand furrows

and filled a thousand granaries

that's what the farm ox did

and who remembers

the poor thin creature

gone weak in the haunches

I like to think

the old ox is content

as he lies sick in the sundown

supposing that the average fellow

is eating well now

夏日绝句

李清照

生当作人杰，

死亦为鬼雄。

至今思项羽，

不肯过江东。

Jueju — a Four-line Poem with Five Words to a Line: Summer

Li Qingzhao

when you are living

be heroic

even dead

stand tall among ghosts

I remember

how Xiang Yu the general

killed himself

rather than

cross the Yangtze for the east

and come back a failure

Xiang Yu (232BC–202BC) was the King of the Western Chu from Suqian, Jiangsu Province. He was surrounded in a battle at He County, Anhui Province but he refused to cross the Yangtze River (Changjiang River) back to his own kingdom as a failure so he killed himself after the fighting.

秋夜将晓出篱门迎凉有感

陆　游

三万里河东入海，

五千仞岳上摩天。

遗民泪尽胡尘里，

南望王师又一年。

Early in the Dawn after an Autumn Night
I Walked beyond the Wattle Gate and Felt
the Cold Air and Had Some Thoughts

Lu You

the river runs thousands of miles

eastward into the sea

peaks five thousands feet high

arch from the foothills to the clouds

common people in the territory the Hu captured

have nothing left but their sorrows

another year goes by and they wonder

when will the Song Kingdom retake this land

Hu is used here to indicate enemy. In history, it was the Jin Dynasty from the northeast who invaded the land of the Song Dynasty, not the real Hu that was in the northwest of the Song Dynasty.

追感往事

陆 游

诸公可叹善谋身，

误国当时岂一秦。

不望夷吾出江左，

新亭对泣亦无人。

Thoughts from Memories

Lu You

silk sops in power

they look out for themselves

at the emperor's court

oh the shame of it

Qin Hui wasn't the only one

who betrayed the dynasty

when the Jin struck us

we won't see the likes of Yi Wu again

that great premier

coming from the east of the Yangtze

I don't imagine these tender skins

care much anyway

they aren't like the men

who wept in Xinting for the lost land

Qin Hui （1090–1155） was the Premier of the Southern Song, from Nanjing City, Jiangsu Province. He insisted on seeking peace talk with the Jin Dynasty to stop Jin's army from marching into the south of the Yangtze River (Changjiang River). He later was labelled a traitor who was responsible for the loss of the north. **Yi Wu** was Guan Zhong （723BC–645BC） from Yingshang, Anhui Province . He was the Premier of the Qi Kingdom and made Qi the strongest among the kingdoms. **Xinting** is in Jiangsu Province. It is on the southern side of the Yangtze River, where high ranking officials cried to each other when they met because the Western Jin Dynasty lost its capital Chang'an （316 AD） and escaped to the south of the Yangtze and they could see the lost land across the river.

示 儿

陆 游

死去元知万事空，

但悲不见九州同。

王师北定中原日，

家祭无忘告乃翁。

To My Sons

Lu You

nothing makes any sense

when a man dies I know

but not seeing the country reunited

this is a real tragedy

the emperor may recapture

the northern interior some day

be sure to tell your father

at his memorial service

十一月四日风雨大作(之二)

陆　游

僵卧孤村不自哀，

尚思为国戍轮台。

夜阑卧听风吹雨，

铁马冰河入梦来。

During a Big Rainstorm on the Fourth Day of the Eleventh Month in the Lunar Calendar (*No.2*)

Lu You

resting stiffly in bed in a lonesome village

I do not feel sad

when I think of going to Luntai

and defending the border for my country

I hear in the darkness

the sound of the wind blowing the rain

and I fall into a dream

of iron-armoured horses on a frozen river

Luntai is on the south of Tianshan Mountain and the north of Tarim Basin. It is under the administration of Xinjiang Uygur Autonomous Region.

梅花绝句 (之二)

陆 游

幽谷那堪更北枝，

年年自分着花迟。

高标逸韵君知否，

正是层冰积雪时。

Jueju — a Four-line Poem with Seven Words to a Line: Plum Blossoms(No. 2)

Lu You

the plum tree is far down in the valley

its branches stretch to the north

you know they can only flower late each year

but you should not take this for granted

those blossoms are noble and unrestrained

when the ice thickens and the snow is deep

横　塘

范成大

南浦春来绿一川，

石桥朱塔两依然。

年年送客横塘路，

细雨垂杨系画船。

Hengtang

Fan Chengda

spring comes once more

south of the river

and the whole world

is a green garden

the stone bridge

and the red pagoda

they are companionable

as always

each year this time

I say goodbye to friends

we walk together

along streets in Hengtang

we see the painted boat

so beautiful in the soft rain

and the willow branches

robed in their ancient silence

Hengtang is in Suzhou City, Jiangsu Province.

寒 雀

杨万里

百千寒雀下空庭，

小集梅梢话晚晴。

特地作团喧杀我，

忽然惊散寂无声。

Sparrows in Winter

Yang Wanli

hundreds of sparrows

crowd the empty courtyard in winter

they puff in their feathers

high on the plum branches

they are saying what a fine evening this is

what a noise they make to disturb me

suddenly they disappear in a startled flock

and the world is as still as death

悯 农

杨万里

稻云不雨不多黄,

荞麦空花早着霜。

已分忍饥度残岁,

更堪岁里闰添长。

Feeling Sad for the Farmers

Yang Wanli

the rice field looks like a rack of clouds

but there wasn't enough rain really

the field has turned yellow in the drought

and the yellow ears have not matured

an early frost nipped the buckwheat

so the farmers have suffered long enough

but there is a thirteenth month in this leap year

and they will suffer longer and how can they

闲居初夏午睡起二绝句(之一)

杨万里

梅子留酸软齿牙，

芭蕉分绿与窗纱。

日长睡起无情思，

闲看儿童捉柳花。

Jueju — a Four-line Poem with Seven Words to a Line: Written after Waking up from a Nap during My Early Summer Vacation

(One of the Two)

Yang Wanli

these purple plums
set your teeth on edge
they are so sour

deep shadows of the banana trees
lend a greener darkness to
the window screen

my heart was at ease
when I awoke on this long day
and my mind becalmed

I watch the children
from where I rest
chasing the willow seeds

道旁店

杨万里

路旁野店两三家，

清晓无汤况有茶。

道是渠侬不好事，

青瓷瓶插紫薇花。

An Inn at the Roadside

Yang Wanli

this road leading from town

two or three inns beside it

you can't get hot water

early in the morning

let alone tea here

the owner of the inn

doesn't attend to his business

well what about these

crape myrtles

all the bright reds

in the blue

celadon ware vases

观书有感

朱　熹

半亩方塘一鉴开，

天光云影共徘徊。

问渠那得清如许，

为有源头活水来。

A Thought as I Read a Book

Zhu Xi

a pond as big as a courtyard

it looks like an uncovered mirror

the bright sky and the clouds

see themselves together in it

I am bewildered trying to explain

how the water can be so clear

a spring-fed creek fills this pond

蚕妇吟

谢枋得

子规啼彻四更时，

起视蚕稠怕叶稀。

不信楼头杨柳月，

玉人歌舞未曾归。

Song from the Woman Who Raises Silkworms

Xie Fangde

cuckoos are already noisy before dawn
the woman gets up to look at the silkworms
she is worried she won't have enough
piles of mulberry leaves for so many

now she finds the moon is down
to the building and the poplars and the willows
and the pretty women who sing and dance
haven't come back to their own homes yet

蚕 妇

张 愈

昨日入城市，

归来泪满巾。

遍身罗绮者，

不是养蚕人。

A Woman Who Raises Silkworms

Zhang Yu

she went into the city yesterday

came home with tears soaking her scarf

people in town who wear silks and satins

are not those who raise silkworms

题临安邸

林 升

山外青山楼外楼，

西湖歌舞几时休。

暖风熏得游人醉，

直把杭州作汴州。

Written on the Wall of the Lin'an Hotel

Lin Sheng

green mountains shadow green mountains

and pavilions trace pavilions

singing and dancing on West Lake

will probably never end

the wind is so warm and gentle

it lulls the tourists into dreams

in dreams they think Hangzhou is

the lost capital Bianzhou

Lin'an is in Hangzhou City today, Zhejiang Province. **Bianzhou** in Kaifeng City, He'nan Province was the capital of the Song Dynasty before they lost the land in the north of the Yangtze River (Changjiang River). **Hangzhou** was the new capital after the Song Dynasty retreated to the south of the Yangtze River.

游园不值

叶绍翁

应怜屐齿印苍苔，

小扣柴扉久不开。

春色满园关不住，

一枝红杏出墙来。

Visiting a Secluded Garden and Learning that the Owner Is Away

Ye Shaoweng

someone trampled the lichen

feeling no pity for those clog marks

I knock at the wattle gate for a while

but no one is home to welcome me

how restless the spring colors are

the door simply cannot shut them in

a red apricot reaches over the fence

with a branch full of blossoms

乡村四月

翁　卷

绿遍山原白满川，

子规声里雨如烟。

乡村四月闲人少，

才了蚕桑又插田。

April in the Country

Weng Juan

all the hills and plains so green
and the white flowers
taking over the valley

the drizzling rain swirls in mist
where the cuckoos sing

you won't see many people
lying around doing nothing
when April warms the countryside

we just went through busy days
with silkworms and mulberry leaves

now we turn and begin
setting out the paddies
with rice seedlings

宋朝词选

The Song Dynasty Lyrics
for Traditional Melodies
960—1279

蝶恋花

柳　永

伫倚危楼风细细，

望极春愁，

黯黯生天际。

草色烟光残照里，

无言谁会凭阑意。

拟把疏狂图一醉，

对酒当歌，

强乐还无味。

衣带渐宽终不悔，

为伊消得人憔悴。

Lines for the Dielianhua Melody

Liu Yong

it is scary standing here so long

at the guarding rail on the upper story

how calm the wind is and subdued

the far horizon is a fountainhead of pain

in the spring sun's waning light

the mountains grow dark

and cast shadows over the green grass

who in the world would understand

how I feel leaning against this rail in silence

I try to forget myself drinking till drunk

we ought to sing when we carouse

but the pretended happiness tastes flat

I feel my clothes are getting baggier

I look more and more wan and pallid

but I don't regret missing her badly

it is worth looking haggard

for a woman you love

渔家傲·秋思

范仲淹

塞下秋来风景异，

衡阳雁去无留意。

四面边声连角起，

千嶂里，

长烟落日孤城闭。

浊酒一杯家万里，

燕然未勒归无计。

羌管悠悠霜满地。

人不寐，

将军白发征夫泪。

Lines for the Yujiaao Melody:
Thoughts of Fall

Fan Zhongyan

the frontier is brooding in autumn

geese are heading to Hengyang

they know it is time to leave

the challenges of military trumpets

echo from valley to valley along the border

the high mountains surround us

long columns of smoke rise in the hills

the sun going down carries away the light

behind the city with the locked gate

soldiers drink wine and feel homesick

there is no victory can be recorded

by carving on rock in Yanran Mountain

and how they can go home

the sound of the Qiang flute never ceases

frost hardens the upland meadows

no one can rest easy in the long nights

and the general's hair turns gray

soldiers posted brush at their tears

Hengyang is in today's Hengyang City, Hu'nan Province. In the local folklore, all geese fly to Hengyang when winter comes. **Yanran Mountain** is in Inner Mongolia today. In the Eastern Han Dynasty, Dou Xian as a commander beat the Huns, and carved his victory on a huge rock in Yanran Mountain. **The Qiang flute** is still a flute with double pipes played by the Qiang ethnic minority group today in the north of Sichuan Province.

苏幕遮

范仲淹

碧云天，

黄叶地。

秋色连波，

波上寒烟翠。

山映斜阳天接水。

芳草无情，

更在斜阳外。

黯乡魂，

追旅思，

夜夜除非，

好梦留人睡。

明月楼高休独倚，

酒入愁肠，

化作相思泪。

Lines for the Sumuzhe Melody

Fan Zhongyan

crystalline clouds and blue pale sky

a shawl of leaves covering the earth

autumn colors in slow waves on the river

cool smoke rises like mist from green waves

mountain like towers of light at day's end

the river in fathoms embraces the sky

now the tender grasses may not miss me

they are far away from this shadowy twilight

but the sweet soul of my native place

follows me wherever I travel

every night every night

I can't sleep without the fancy dreams

simply don't climb to the upper floors alone

when the moon glimmers overhead

and the white liqueur that a man drinks

increases the sorrow he already knows

and abandons him to his lovesick tears

踏莎行

晏　殊

小径红稀，

芳郊绿遍。

高台树色阴阴见。

春风不解禁杨花，

蒙蒙乱扑行人面。

翠叶藏莺，

朱帘隔燕，

炉香静逐游丝转。

一场愁梦酒醒时，

斜阳却照深深院。

Lines for the Tasuoxing Melody

Yan Shu

flowers begin to fade

along the path border

the beautiful field is entirely green

trees in full leaf

deep and dark comfort your eyes

when you look down on them

from the lofty balcony

and in the spring wind

catkins floating from the poplars

blunder against the faces of people

as they walk the streets

orioles go to the jade green trees

and find their hiding places

the vermilion curtain hung at the door

keeps the inquisitive swallows out

the fragrance of an incense burner

permeates the air

I have been asleep after drinking

now awake from a sad dream

and observe long bars of sunlight

slanting deep into the courtyard

浣溪沙

晏 殊

一曲新词酒一杯，

去年天气旧亭台。

夕阳西下几时回？

无可奈何花落去，

似曾相识燕归来。

小园香径独徘徊。

Lines for the Huanxisha Melody

Yan Shu

sipping a cup of wine

I compose a new song

the weather is the same

as last year

and the pavilion too

but the setting sun

seems never to come back

we can't do very much

about the flowers falling

and yet the swallows return

it seems familiar as ever

and so I enjoy

the fragrance of this little garden

walking back and forth

on the graceful path

sentimental and alone

采桑子

晏　殊

时光只解催人老，

不信多情，

长恨离亭。

泪滴春衫酒易醒。

梧桐昨夜西风急，

淡月胧明，

好梦频惊。

何处高楼雁一声？

Lines for the Caisangzi Melody

Yan Shu

time doesn't care about anything

except making a man old in a hurry

why do we have such tender feelings

why is it so painful

saying goodbye to old friends

I drink to cure my lovesickness

then I wake with a shirt stained with tears

the wind blew hard from the west last night

it shook the parasol trees and jarred the leaves

the moon was so pale I thought it would vanish

a happy dream ends when it should not

and then there was that one sound only

that sudden long lonesome cry of a lost goose

from on top of this building or that one

蝶恋花

晏　殊

槛菊愁烟兰泣露

罗幕轻寒，

燕子双飞去。

明月不谙离别苦，

斜光到晓穿朱户。

昨夜西风凋碧树，

独上高楼，

望尽天涯路。

欲寄彩笺兼尺素，

山阔水长知何处？

Lines for the Dielianhua Melody

Yan Shu

chrysanthemums outside the guardrails

look sad in the hazy blue mist

dewdrops sprinkle the orchids

like so many lost tears

air at night chills the curtains

swallows abandon the house two by two

well the gleaming moon

doesn't feel the pain of departure

it floods this huge house painted red

all night long with its cold beams

the wind out of the west

withered the green trees last night

now I climb alone

to the upper story of this house

and watch the road leading to the horizon

I want to send you poems and a letter

but the mountain ranges

and the wide rivers divide us

蝶恋花

欧阳修

庭院深深深几许？

杨柳堆烟，

帘幕无重数。

玉勒雕鞍游冶处，

楼高不见章台路。

雨横风狂三月暮，

门掩黄昏，

无计留春住。

泪眼问花花不语，

乱红飞过秋千去。

Lines for the Dielianhua Melody

Ouyang Xiu

who knows how deep the courtyards are

poplar and willow trees roil like smoke

there are many curtains in those halls

too many to count

halters with silver inlays

and finely carved saddles

belonging to men who come for comfort

I can't see those houses in Zhangtai Street

although my mansion commands a fine view

the wind is savage in late march

it drives the rain before it

the door is closing as the evening darkens

but springtime goes whatever way it will

my eyes are full of tears

they question the blossoms but get no answer

only clouds of red petals drifting by the swing

Zhangtai Street referred to places in the Han Dynasty where the street was lined up on both sides with brothels.

玉楼春

欧阳修

尊前拟把归期说，

未语春容先惨咽。

人生自是有情痴，

此恨不关风与月。

离歌且莫翻新阕，

一曲能叫肠寸结。

直须看尽洛城花，

始共春风容易别。

Lines for the Yulouchun Melody

Ouyang Xiu

I would have made something up

about seeing her again

but just when I was getting started

her lovely face clouded

and she choked back her tears

people are always heartsick

from one thing or another

this has nothing to do with wind and moon

don't sing old farewell songs to new lyrics

it'll give you lot of pain in your stomach

and anyway as soon as you have enjoyed

all flowers in Luo City

it won't be so hard

saying goodbye to a breeze in the spring

Luo City is in Luoyang, on the northern shore of the Luo River, He'nan Province.

念奴娇·赤壁怀古

苏 轼

大江东去，

浪淘尽，

千古风流人物。

故垒西边，

人道是，

三国周郎赤壁。

乱石崩云，

惊涛裂岸，

卷起千堆雪。

江山如画，

一时多少豪杰！

遥想公瑾当年，

小乔初嫁了，

雄姿英发。

羽扇纶巾，

谈笑间，

强虏灰飞烟灭。

故国神游，

多情应笑我，

早生华发。

人间如梦，

一尊还酹江月。

Lines for the Niannujiao Melody: Recalling Old Times at Chibi

Su Shi

the great river courses to the east

many famous people

have been washed away by waves

during the long history of this land

west of the rocks

people say it is in Chibi

Zhou Yu won a battle in the Three Kingdoms

jumbled boulders

fall onto the bank of the river there

like clouds breaking into pieces

and powerful breakers charge with a roar

thousands of big rolling snowstorms of surf

eager to wrench the bank down

the landscape is a breathtaking painting

where so many heroes had their day

remember now what year it was

when general Zhou Yu was young

he married the younger one of the Qiao sisters

he looked so handsome and commanding

holding the feather fan

and wearing the black stole

just standing there all talk and laughter

while the strong invaders were burned to ashes

they vanished like smoke

well people may smile at my early gray hair

and my overwrought feeling

as I visit the site of the Three Kingdoms

I know that life is a vanished dream

I bow to the moon in the river

and pour out a glass of wine to show my respect

Chibi is in the southeast of Hubei Province and on the south of the Yangtze River (Changjiang River), where during the Three Kingdoms the allied forces of the Wu and Shu Kingdoms crushed the force of the Wei Kingdom by setting its fleet on fire. The wind from east in Chibi that night was in great favour of the Wu and Shu. **Three Kingdoms** are the Wei, Shu and Wu, existed from 220 to 280. **General Zhou** was Zhou Yu, the commander of the army in Wu. He was born in Shu County, Anhui Province, in 175, and died in Yueyang City, Hu'nan Province, in 210. **The Qiao sisters** were from Qianshan, Anhui Province, who were well-known beautiful women during the Three Kingdoms time. The younger one was born in 180 and married Zhou Yu in 196.

水调歌头

丙辰中秋，欢饮达旦，大醉，作此篇，兼怀子由。

苏　轼

明月几时有？

把酒问青天。

不知天上宫阙，

今夕是何年？

我欲乘风归去，

又恐琼楼玉宇，

高处不胜寒。

起舞弄清影，

何似在人间。

转朱阁，

低绮户，

照无眠。

不应有恨，

何事长向别时圆？

人有悲欢离合，

月有阴晴圆缺，

此事古难全。

但愿人长久，

千里共婵娟。

Lines for the Shuidiaogetou Melody

At the Mid-Autumn Festival in 1076, drank until morning, got smashed

then I wrote these lines for missing Ziyou.

Su Shi

how many times does a man see the gleaming moon

round itself in the heavens

I am holding a cup of wine

and asking this of the sky

I don't know what year this is

in the palace of stars

I wanted to return there

sailing on the wind

but I am afraid

that dwelling of shining jade is a place

too high and too cold for me

so I stand here and dance with my shadow

it is better to live an earthbound life

the moon slowly circles the red-painted pavilion

its beams slant into my room

I cannot sleep in that pale light

although I want to believe

the moon is no enemy of ours

and yet why is it always at the full

when we suffer the pain of exile

it is true we know happiness as well as sorrow

and go away and return

and the moon is often shadowed in cloud

and it is often shining

and full sometimes and sometimes crescent

nevertheless it has not been easy

struggling to be satisfied

not since the old days

but I wish you a long life

and the joy of sharing the graceful moon

even though a thousand miles separate us

少年游

晏几道

离多最是，

东西流水，

终解两相逢。

浅情纵似，

行云无定，

犹到梦魂中。

可怜人意，

薄于云水，

佳会更难重。

细想从来，

断肠多处，

不与这番同！

Lines for the Shaonianyou Melody

Yan Jidao

what is it that suffers the most

from a separation

water runs east and water runs west

but water will become one with itself again

what is it that suffers the most

from a loss of feeling

clouds drift across the wind

without particular attraction

but a small loving dream

will join them together once more

people don't care about each other

what a shame what a shame

they are not as constant as water and clouds

and as for happy reunions

there are not so many of them

I think about these things

pondering on them over and over

I have known disappointment before

and it was pretty bad

but this parting wrenches my heart

鹊桥仙

秦 观

纤云弄巧，

飞星传恨，

银汉迢迢暗度。

金风玉露一相逢，

便胜却人间无数。

柔情似水，

佳期如梦，

忍顾鹊桥归路！

两情若是久长时，

又岂在朝朝暮暮！

Lines for the Queqiaoxian Melody

Qin Guan

these transparent clouds so delicate

that falling star carries regret like a messenger

the Milky Way so luminous a star vanishes in it

for the cowherd and the woman at the loom

Altair and Vega

those lovers who can meet only one night in a year

but for them this is more wonderful

than the countless times

lovers in this world meet

they are joined for one long perfected moment

they merge into each other like slow running waters

their happy loving is the kindliest of dreams

they have to know the sadness of looking back

as they depart on their separate ways

traveling over the bridge of soaring magpies

but because what they feel shines in them forever

it surely does not distress them

each day and each night they cannot be together

Altair and Vega: the cowherd (**Altair**) married the fairy maiden from the heavens (**Vega**) in a Chinese legend, but after giving birth to two children the fairy maiden was taken away by the soldiers sent by the King of the heavens. With the help of a piece of skin offered by a cow he flew up to the sky with their two children to chase after her but he couldn't cross over the Silver River (the Milky Way). As a result they were allowed to meet once a year in the evening on the seventh day of the seventh month in the lunar calendar. Since then magpies gather on top of the Silver River to form a bridge with their wings in that evening. This helps the couple, mother and children with their short reunion.

如梦令

李清照

昨夜雨疏风骤，

浓睡不消残酒。

试问卷帘人，

却道海棠依旧。

知否？知否？

应是绿肥红瘦！

Lines for the Rumengling Melody

Li Qingzhao

it hardly rained
but the wind blew like crazy
last night

I feel the wine this morning
although my sleep was dreamless

now the maid comes in
and I question her
as she rolls the window shade

she says the crab apples
are the same as yesterday

you ought to know
you ought to know
they should look much greener
and a lot less red

满江红

岳 飞

怒发冲冠，

凭栏处，

潇潇雨歇。

抬望眼，

仰天长啸，

壮怀激烈。

三十功名尘与土，

八千里路云和月。

莫等闲，

白了少年头，

空悲切。

靖康耻，

犹未雪。

臣子恨，

何时灭！

驾长车，

踏破贺兰山阙。

壮志饥餐胡虏肉，

笑谈渴饮匈奴血。

待从头，

收拾旧山河，

朝天阙。

Lines for the Manjianghong Melody

Yue Fei

I am so angry my scalp prickles under my hat

I grip the rail until my knuckles turn white

waiting for this pouring rain to stop

I stare straight up

and howl at the sky

oh I am torn into pieces in my gut

here I am thirty years old

honour and fame are mud and dust

I have fought for the dynasty

eight thousand miles under the clouds and the moon

you can't just sit here and do nothing

what value are regrets when your hair goes gray

when are we going to make good the insult

the Jin invaders gave us

when they captured our emperor

when are those of us in power going to avenge

the disgrace of losing our dynasty

we should take to the war chariots

and careen through the passes in the Helan Mountain

we are so determined to fight

we have to beat this war white hot again

ready to eat their flesh when we hunger

we laugh and talk over victories

ready to drink their blood to slake our thirst

raise our banners in the lost territory once more

the old capital waits for the emperor

Helan Mountain lies between Ningxia Hui Autonomous Region and Inner Mongolia Autonomous Region. Its major peak is located in the northwest of Yinchuan City. The old capital was Bianjing, which is Kaifeng City today in He'nan Province. It was captured later by the Jin invaders in 1127. The Song Dynasty retreated to the south of the Yangtze River.

钗头凤

陆　游

红酥手，

黄藤酒，

满城春色宫墙柳。

东风恶，

欢情薄。

一怀愁绪，

几年离索。

错！错！错！

春如旧，

人空瘦，

泪痕红悒鲛绡透。

桃花落，

闲池阁。

山盟虽在，

锦书难托。

莫！莫！莫！

Lines for the Chaitoufeng Melody

Lu You

you offered me the yellow wine

holding it in your slender pink hands

the town was filled with flowers

and the willows were in leaf

at the red walls of the palace

and then that cruel east wind

came howling like some insane thing

and the world of love fell before it

oh the sorrow is down deep in my heart

for years we were parted and lonely

wrong

it is wrong

it is all wrong

now it is springtime again in the

but you are thin and worn for a reason

and tears streak your make-up

and stain your silk handkerchief

the peach blossoms have already fallen

the pond and the pavilion

not so many visit them now

we made a solemn pledge of our love

and that is still true in our hearts

but I cannot even send you a fond letter

oh no

it cannot be

it is impossible

卜算子·咏梅

陆 游

驿外断桥边，

寂寞开无主。

已是黄昏独自愁，

更著风和雨。

无意苦争春，

一任群芳妒。

零落成泥碾作尘，

只有香如故。

Lines for the Busuanzi Melody:
an Ode to Plum Blossoms

Lu You

beyond the inn

alongside the ancient bridge

you are the solitary

the blossoms no one owns

you are the lonesome one

when sundown sadness

goes deeper still with cold rain

and a raw whip in the wind

no matter you do not seek

a spring loveliness

you do not bother those flowers

that compete for beauty

you will fall in the mire

and be trampled into dust

but the delicate fragrance of yours

will forever be there as before

夜游宫·记梦寄师伯浑

陆 游

雪晓清笳乱起。

梦游处，

不知何地。

铁骑无声望似水。

想关河，

雁门西，

青海际。

睡觉寒灯里。

漏声断，

月斜窗纸。

自许封候在万里。

有谁知，

鬓虽残，

心未死。

Lines for the Yeyougong Melody:
Writing about a Dream
and Sending the Note to Shi Bohun

Lu You

many northern reed flutes are played

here and there in the snowy dawn

I locate this some place in my dream

I don't know where it is

the armoured soldiers on horses are hushed

they are to move like a tidal wave

I am thinking of mountain passes and rivers

the west beyond Yanmen

and the places along Qinghai

I wake up in the dim light of the lamp

it is a late hour toward morning

the sand has stopped running in the hourglass

and the last light of the moon

glistens on the paper-covered windows

once I had hoped to recover the lost territory

who could have predicted this

my hair is gray now and thin

but my heart is still as tense as a bowstring

Shi Bohun was from Meishan, Sichuan Province, who was a hermit, a poet and a well-known writer but refused to serve the government. His other name was Shi Hunfu. He was a good friend of Lu You who wrote the preface for *Shi Bohun's Collected Works*. Yanmen referred to Yanmen Pass built on the Yanmen Mountain, which is in Dai County, Shanxi Province. Qinghai is Qinhai Lake, in Qinhai Province, occupying the northern part of the Qinghai-Tibet Plateau.

菩萨蛮·书江西造口壁

辛弃疾

郁孤台下清江水，

中间多少行人泪。

西北望长安，

可怜无数山。

青山遮不住，

毕竟东流去。

江晚正愁余，

山深闻鹧鸪。

Lines for the Pusaman Melody: Written on the Cliffs at Zaokou in Jiangxi Province

Xin Qiji

the Qing River runs

below the Yugutai Hills

it is swollen with tears

of those miserable travellers

I look northwest for Chang'an

what a sad thing

there are so many mountains

between me and that city

rivers dash to the east

what are green mountains to them

nothing can block their way

as twilight darkens the water

I am deep in thoughts with worries

but off in the hills

calls of francolins sound like

it isn't right to do.

Zaokou is in Wan'an County, Jiangxi Province, and the cliff is on the western shore of the Gan River. The Qing River (Qingjiang River) here indicates the river running beside Yugutai. Yugutai is on the top of Helan Mountain, in Ganzhou City, Jiangxi Province.

青玉案·元夕

辛弃疾

东风夜放花千树，

更吹落，

星如雨。

宝马雕车香满路，

凤箫声动，

玉壶光转，

一夜鱼龙舞。

蛾儿雪柳黄金缕，

笑语盈盈暗香去。

众里寻他千百度。

蓦然回首，

那人却在，

灯火阑珊处。

Lines for the Qingyu'an Melody:
the Lantern Festival

Xin Qiji

as if the east wind blew the trees

into blossom that night by the thousands

as if even the heavens were shaken down

the lanterns look like a shower of stars

and there are prized horses and finely carved carts

passing through the crowded streets

the streets are rich with fragrance

and the beautiful sounds of small reeds and flutes

the moon shaped lanterns

flash multicoloured lights

lanterns shaped like fish and some like dragons

the revellers dance with all night long

women have their hair bound with ornaments

fashioned of spun gold thread

they trail the delicate aromas of flowers

as they walk by joking and laughing

and I looked for her all through the festival

a hundred times until suddenly I glanced back

and saw where she stood alone in that place

where one or two lanterns still burned

鹧鸪天

有客慨然谈功名，因追念少年时事，戏作。

辛弃疾

壮岁旌旗拥万夫，

锦襜突骑渡江初。

燕兵夜娖银胡䩮，

汉箭朝飞金仆姑。

追往事，

叹今吾。

春风不染白髭须。

却将万字平戎策，

换得东家种树书。

Lines for the Zhegutian Melody

After a guest talked about fame and honour with me, I recalled deeds of my
own when I was young, and wrote this poem to pass away the time.

Xin Qiji

what fine years they were to remember

the imperial troops by the thousands

massing around the battle flags

all of us in tight silk colors

urging our stallions across the river

that was when the Jin invaders slept

with silver-studded quivers for pillows

they could hear the thudding of horses

from six valleys over

but our cavalry shocked them

with the deadly zinging of Jinpugu arrows

when I think about those campaigns

I am sickened by what goes on now

it was never a spring wind

that turned my beard and moustache gray

I have written suggestions to the court

by the cartload with good advice

for beating the invaders back

but my efforts have brought me no thanks

just a handful of books here

telling me how to plant trees

Jin invaders were from the Jin Dynasty(1115–1234), in the northeast of China which invaded the Song Dynasty. Jinpugu was a brand of arrow, which was from a legend that anybody can become a sharp shooter by using arrows from this brand.

后 记

——论中国古诗词英译

当代的翻译事业相当繁荣,然而在翻译理论的研究上却出现了某些困境,这一点在中国古诗词英译领域表现尤为突出。

困境产生的主要原因是在翻译中同时强调两个方面:"再创造"和"忠实原文"。因而可以通过的夹缝越来越小。

中国翻译界长期以来受"信、达、雅"三字的困扰:"达"与"雅"明显表示"再创造","信"表示"忠实原文"。当这两点同时强调到极点时,译家就会面临巨大的挑战,甚至"在劫难逃"。德国翻译家阿尔弗莱德·库勒拉(1895—1975)用荷马史诗——《奥德赛》中守护在那个极窄的麦斯纳海峡两岸上的两个怪物——一个用六头三排牙把人吃掉,一个用旋涡把船弄翻——来比喻上述两点,"一个是斯茨拉,一个是哈里布达,我们应该像奥德赛一样驾上一条小船从它们中间穿过"①。他提出了目标,但问题是如何实现。人神皆知那是一个任何船都无法通过的海峡,可是奥德赛的船却能险中取胜。

----

① 王育伦:《翻译好比……》,《翻译通讯》1984 年第 11 期。

　　实际上，翻译并不是再创造，只是再现，最多是创造性地再现；而这个"创造性"又只能局限于为了再现所需要的译者的独创性。文学作品中的情节、人物、地点、背景、对话、叙述人、感情、形象、风格，都只能是原作者创造的，译家只能再现这一切。但是，再现过程中难免遇到由于语言和文化的差异造成的不可译处，译家也得发挥一些创造性，但目的是更好地再现。如果译家不甘寂寞，一定要对原著加以增删和杂以自己的想象，那也不是再创造，而是对原著以另一种文字进行改写，这当然不是翻译。

　　发挥创造精神说的是译家的主体性，并非指译家以较强主体精神翻译的作品便是再创造的作品。这种主体精神的发挥也必须限于"翻译"二字的语义范畴之内。作家茅盾同志说过这样的话："文学翻译是用另一种语言，把原作的艺术意境传达出来，使读者在读译文的时候能像读原作一样得到启发、感动和美的感受。"①即便在译文中实现了这种意境，也只是传达而不是再创造。

　　"忠实于原文"是忠实于原文所表达的内容和美感。"信"字的内涵也只能到此为止。长期以来，翻译界有一种过分强调对文学作品的语言形式忠实的倾向。理由是内容与形式应当统一，一定的内容要求一定的文学形式和语言形式；不忠实于原文的语言形式就不可能完全表达原文的内容。这种理论使文学翻译中的诗歌翻译，特别是中国古诗词英译尤其困难。

①《俄文教学》1954 年第 12 期。

　　诗歌语言以其丰富的内蕴引起无尽的联想,其本身就是难以把握的,尤其是古典诗歌。早在汉朝,董仲舒(公元前179年—公元前104年)在说到对当时的古典诗歌《诗经》的五花八门的解读时就说"诗无达诂"。由此可见,诗歌翻译的"信"——忠实于原文——在很大程度上取决于译者对原诗的理解与对译语和译语文化的把握,及其再现原语诗的美感的能力。这里就有很大程度的理解上的不同。这种理解的不同不仅仅指文字还指诗的形象思维的内涵。它们有时甚至是弦外之音,也就是只能意会不能言传的东西。从文学欣赏的角度来看,人们对于诗的理解也不断地演变,由此,建立在理解程度上的"信"不可能有一个一成不变的标准。

　　除此之外,诗歌翻译在两个方面面临比其他翻译更大的挑战:语言的不可译性和文化的不可译性。英汉两种语言在句子结构、词形、发音和表达方式上都完全不同。英语是拼音文字,汉语是象形和表意文字。这不仅造成语言的表层形式的不同,也造成语言的深层结构的迥异。诗歌作为语言艺术文学尤其讲求语言,而中国古诗词对于语言的讲求可谓达到了顶峰。英语国家与中国在文化背景上也截然不同。不同文化背景,也造成作品自身具有不可译文化。

　　面对这样严肃的挑战和接近于无的夹缝,中国古诗词英译也必须做出自己的选择,那就是摈弃复制诗歌形式和语言形式的追求,译出中国古诗词的独具民族文化特色的美感。宋淇先生说:"文学作品,尤其是第一流的文学作品,是创作者心血的结晶,翻译者的责任无非在传达它的意旨,而且还要顾及意指背后的境界，作者使用文字的风格，可以意会而不可言传的神韵、气魄等抽象概念。"① 这句话的核心在于强调传达意旨，展显神韵。

做出这一选择无疑是痛苦的。中国古诗词是中国传统文化中举世无双的璀璨瑰宝，对于它的诗歌形式和语言形式读者都有一种难以舍弃的感情。我们尤其为中国古诗词中的空灵、意象、真情与和谐而骄傲于世。然而，当我们翻译中国古诗词时，我们必然考虑：为什么要翻译它们。中国古诗词英译的目的就是要把中国的文化瑰宝展示给英语世界，而不是将其翻译成英语后自己欣赏。可是古诗词英译的特点与我们译入英语古典诗歌有区别。英文多数是两个音节以上的词，而汉语是单音节词。将英语古诗译为汉语可以有照顾节奏韵律的较大回旋余地，而中国古诗词英译，则与上述情况相反。中国古诗词用字精炼，讲究用典，不仅有韵和节拍，又加有平仄，这成了几乎不可能在另一种语言里再现的难度。长期以来我们较侧重英译汉的许多规律的研究，所幸近年来关于中国古诗词英译的研究兴起，不幸的是又过于强调对诗歌形式和语言形式方面的忠实，这严重束缚了中国古诗词英译的发展。

中国古诗词英译介绍了中国的传统文化，使其在全世界被认知，同时对世界文学产生影响。赵毅衡教授的专著《远游的诗神 中国古典诗歌对美国新诗运动的影响》②里充分缕析了这一文学现

---

① 宋淇（林以亮）：《文学作品举隅》，香港中文大学出版社，1983。

② 赵毅衡：《远游的诗神 中国古典诗歌对美国新诗运动的影响》，四川人民出版社，1985。

象,大量举证说明中国古典诗歌如何影响,以及在多大程度上影响了美国的新诗运动。他为证实这一点做出了巨大的贡献。 同时对中国古诗词英译提出了精辟的看法,他指出,为了形式、为了韵律会使诗的意义的传递蒙受危害。他对用英语自由体诗翻译中国古典诗词的见解独到。美国诗人庞德,新诗运动的重要成员, 在美国二十世纪初新诗运动兴起时就预言中国古典诗歌将对二十世纪美国诗歌产生巨大影响。[1]美国新诗运动的另一个重要成员玛丽安·莫尔认为新诗就是来自中国诗。[2]

从对美国二十世纪初的新诗运动产生深远影响和对二十世纪五十年代后的英美诗歌产生巨大影响的中国古诗词英译来看,不难看出,大部分是不拘泥诗歌形式和语言形式的译作。其中的原因是很明显的,因为中国古典诗词的诗歌形式到二十世纪初已经基本上不再使用,它的节拍和韵律规定都已经不复存在于现代诗之中。作为母语读者的中国人,也有相当大一部分人是靠对古诗词的翻译和注释来欣赏其诗美了。这期间,英语诗的传统格律也基本上被扬弃了,特别是二十世纪初,新诗在美国兴起后,传统格律诗虽时有人写,然而已经不可能成为气候了。当然,它不像在中国那么彻底,因为中国经历了一次从文言文向白话文转变的过程, 导致传统格律更加彻底地被忘却。

---

[1] *Poetry*,1959(2):227.

[2] *New Poetry since 1912, Anthology of Magazine Verse*, 1926, p.1174.

翻译的本质就是传递信息——内容信息和美感信息——而对于翻译诗词来说，问题是怎样传递美感信息，即怎样译出诗的内在美。古诗词的外在诗美——诗的形式和诗的语言形式——在中国古典诗词中也确实曾起到很大的作用，主要是在音韵方面。然而这种音韵美在英译中是无法表达的。

人们曾尝试用抑扬格来表示平仄，用重读音节与中国古诗词中的字数相对，用强调韵的密度来对应中国古诗词中的韵等等。这实质上都是徒劳的。因为这种解决办法只能得到相似的效果，并未真实地反映出原诗的诗歌形式和语言形式。相似并不等于是。我们说格式大体整齐，其实是不整齐；我们说大体表现原韵，其实是不同于原韵。有一则幽默说，一个男孩子得了奖，原因是在回答老师的问题"鸵鸟有几只腿？"时，别的孩子都说有四只，而只有他说有三只，老师奖励他，是因为他的答案更接近正确。

有人担心，把中国古诗词都译成"散文释义"会使外国人误解，以为中国古诗词就是这种样子。那么弄成相似的形式不是也同样会导致误解吗？另外，在人们看来是"散文化释义"，而实际上是一首不错的英文无韵诗。如果它译出了原诗的意境、神韵、美感，它就是一首好的译诗。而且它会被英语读者接受，加以欣赏，甚至参与再创造，加深对诗美的享受和感应。

在长期的欣赏活动中，欣赏群体形成了一种欣赏走向和欣赏心理，如果译诗不与这种欣赏标准吻合，便很难被接受。我们强调的语言形式与内容不可分恰恰会造成灾难。难怪一些英语读者，无法理解过分忠实于古诗词的外在美的译诗的诗美，甚至怀疑那是诗。不考虑欣赏群体意识,译诗难以成功。

　　作为一名母语为汉语的中国古诗词译者,尤其要谨记这一点。我们在英诗汉译时,译者本人就是欣赏群体的代表,清楚地知道在译出内容与美感的同时怎样才能在译诗形式上被接受。然而,在把中国古诗词英译时,我们往往过多地考虑如何保留我们的古诗词的形式美,否则无颜以对祖宗;殊不知,这样一来,我们祖先创作的如同明净夜空中灿烂群星般的古诗词,却难以传扬海外。真正在海外流行的,还是那些被我们贬低为不"信"的译本。它们的功绩非同小可。在本族语中能够有助于表现诗的内在美的外形,在译入另一种文化框架下的语言中时,必须做出适应新的框架的外形变化,否则译文就会受到译语文化的排拒,而使译诗的目的落空。我认为,在原语中诗歌形式和诗歌的内容是相互协调的,但若把形式原封不动地搬入译语文化中,他们就可能变为相互对立和冲突的,因为原语文化的传统格局决定了内容对形式的选择。选择是针对原语文化熏陶下的原语读者来说的。同样的内容在不同的文化圈里,也会选择不同的形式。就是同一内容在同一语言文化中,由于创作者自身的文化修养和对读者的考虑不同,也会对形式做出不同的选择。所以内容与形式的统一也不是绝对的。

　　在当代的英美,诗歌的流变令人眼花缭乱。如果你以朗费罗的诗歌形式和语言形式为参照创作,那毫无疑问是落伍的;如果以弗罗斯特为参照创作,也许还会有些读者,但肯定不会多;就连意象派也在"独领风骚十几年"后"销声匿迹"了。我们要参照的必定是接受了各种流变的特色，并还在不断创新的当代诗。不要担心这种译本不会持久，由流变到扬弃是历史必然，将来必定会有人译出更能为那个时代的欣赏者所能接受的译本。然而历史和传统又总是有它们自身的脉络可寻，纵观世界翻译史，往往是那些在当时就为欣赏群体所能接受的译本才具有较为持久的价值。

　　只有当内在美不受外在的形式的干扰，译出来的诗才能传达出原诗的真髓——内容和美感。任何诗的外在美都是为内在美服务的，是为了外化内在美才存在的。如果只坚持忠实于原语诗的外形，让外在美成为内在美外化的障碍，其得失便不难权衡。更为不幸的是在努力忠实于外形，表现无法再现的外表美时，产生了对内在美的忽略甚至损害。这种损害又常常不易被发现，特别不容易被目的语读者发现。由此，过分强调外在美的做法就会堂而皇之地"登堂入室"。李锡胤教授在举"推敲"一词的故事为例时写道："译成另一种语言时，偶尔找到巧妙地方法曲折地传达出原作的细微语言特点，固然令人拍案叫绝，但'未可以明召大号，以绳天下之梅也'，一则不同的语言各有巧妙不同，勉强为之，学力不足者容易刻鹄类鹜；二则即使译者心知其忌，苦心传达，读者未必'领情'。"①

　　这一问题在中国古诗词英译中是一个突出的问题，在其他文学形式的翻译中也普遍存在。我认为当前国际翻译界中的交际

---

① 李锡胤：《对翻译的思考》，《外语学刊》1987 年第 2 期。

学派的观点更看重实际。他们主张翻译的重点要放在尽量以信息接受者所能理解和欣赏的形式来传译原文的意义。他们强调信息接受者——语言交流过程的目的方——的重要作用。换句话说，就是考虑译文对译文读者能否像原文对原文读者一样产生审美刺激，引起诗的共鸣。但是必须强调，从一个文化框架向另一个文化框架转化时，不能转化文化内容。例如："把英语句子'It (something) is as significant (to me) as a game of cricket' (这事如同板球一样重要) 译成法语，译文应为'C'estaussisignificantif que de faire de la course de velo'(这事如同自行车赛一样重要)，译成汉语则应是'这事如同吃饭一样重要'。"① 这样一来就不是使译文形式与译文文化融合，而是使信息内涵根据译文文化改变。这是超越译家权力范围的行为，因为译文改变了原文的创造内容，它不再是翻译而是改写了。那么西方美人的金发碧眼，是否要换成云鬓若乌云，加明眸皓齿；孙中山是否也要换成华盛顿；那首著名的歌曲《龙的传人》译成英文，龙字是否也要换成什么呢？因为龙在汉语里有兴旺发达和吉祥如意之意，而在英语中却象征危险可怕与凶恶暴力。这种做法已不是试图在两种语言和两种文化之间架起沟通的桥，而是超越不同语言和文化的界限去实现意指的传递，这必然会走向"因形害义"之路，而且会堵塞不同文化交融与吸收其他文化中的语言的渠道。

这中间有一个"度"，掌握好这个"度"就会架起诗的内涵美

---

① 潭载喜、尤金·奈达：《论翻译学的途径》，《外语教学与研究》1987 年第 1 期。

得以过渡的桥——差异语言文化的连接点。问题是要承认翻译的局限性。中国古诗词的外在美无法在英译中再现，是语言所具有的不同民族文化、心理和历史的差异决定的。我们只能充分运用英语语言来再现中国古诗词的内涵美。有一个经常为人引用的故事，一个画家被非难未画出海伦的美却画出了海伦的富有。画家辩解说，绘画艺术是有局限的，我恪守这种局限应受到褒奖。①

王守义

写于 1986 年 5 月

改写于 1987 年 9 月

再改写于 2018 年 8 月

于多伦多教堂街

---

① 莱辛：《拉奥孔》，朱光潜译，人民文学出版社，1979。

Epilogue

— On the Translation of Chinese Classical Poems into English

The prosperity of the cause of today's translation is quite impressive, while some dilemmas in the study of the theories in translation are causing concerns now, among which the theory on the translation of Chinese classical poems into English is extremely confusing.

The dilemma was created by the emphases on "re-creation" and "loyalty to the original text" at the same time, therefore the space between them becomes so narrow that it is hard to pass through.

The art of translation in China has long been impeded by the dilemma caused by the following three terms: "faithfulness, expressiveness, and elegance." Obviously, "expressiveness and elegance" indicate "re-creation," but "faithfulness" indicates "loyalty to the original text." When these two aspects are both stressed to the extreme translators may face serious challenges and possibly are bound to failure. German translator Alfred Kurella (1895 – 1975) attempted to compare the two aspects mentioned above with the two monsters, one of which capsizes ships with a whirlpool and the other of which just eats up human beings with its six heads, three rows of teeth in each, guarding on opposite sides of a very narrow channel — Strait of Messina in Homer's epic — *Odyssey*: "One is Scylla and the other is Charybdis. We should row our boat like Odysseus to pass through between them." [①] He's set up the standard, but the question is how we can make it. Although it's known by both gods and men that no ship could sail through the strait but the ship of Odysseus' survived all the risks.

As a matter of fact, translation is not to recreate but to reproduce only, and to the most it is to reproduce in a creative way. Somehow the "creative way" should be limited to the needs of the translator's originality in the reproduction. Everything in a literary work was initially created by the original author, such as the plot, character, location, environment, dialogue, narrator, emotion, image and style. For all of these, what the translator can do is only to reproduce; but in the process of the reproduction possibly there are some difficulties caused by the differences between the language and culture, which are likely impossible to translate. In such cases, a translator sometimes is bound to apply his / her own creativity but only to do a better reproduction. If a translator is not pleased with the limitation

---

① Wang Yulun, "Translation Is Like...," *Chinese Translators Journal,* 1984(11):40.

he or she may be determined to cut something off from the original or to insert the translator's own imagination. This is still not to recreate but to rewrite the original with the target language. And thus, it can't be classified as translation.

To bring the initiative of the translator into play means to gain the translator's individuality; however, it doesn't imply that a translation with strong individuality of the translator's is a piece of literary work recreated by the translator. The enhancement of a translator's individuality should also be limited into the frame of the semantic meaning of the word "translation." A famous Chinese writer Mao Dun once commented: "Literary translation is to relay the mood and tone of the original literary work using another language. When readers read the translation text they'll get the same enlightenment, the same touching, and the same aesthetic appeal as they read in their own language." [1] Even though the translation achieves this it is still a relay not a re-creation.

"Loyalty to the original" should mean loyalty to what the text expresses and its aesthetic perception. The implication of the "Faithfulness" cannot go any further than this. The tendency of over stressing the faithfulness to the form of language in the original for literary translation has long been present in the art of literary

---

[1] *Russian Teaching*, 1954(12).

translation. The argument is that unification of form and content is required. Thus, a certain content requires a certain literary form and a certain form of language. Therefore, the translation will not be able to carry out the content of the original text if the translators fail to be faithful to the language form in the original. The theory of unification of form and content has made it very difficult to translate a poem, and to translate Chinese classical poems into English in particular.

The language used in poetry is distinguished by its rich implications that trigger endless associated thinking. The language in poems, especially in classical poems itself is hard to comprehend in its totality. As early in the Han Dynasty Mr. Dong Zhongshu (179 BC – 104 BC) wrote while talking about the variety of explanations to *Shi Jing,* the ancient poems at that time , "No explanations to classical poems could be perfect and standard." It's a common understanding that in translating poems the faithfulness — the loyalty to the original — depends on to what extent the translator has gained understanding of the original poem, mastery of the target language and the target culture and the ability to reproduce the aesthetic appeal of the original poem. There is a great difference in understanding for different people, which means not only the understanding of words but also the understanding of the implications conveyed by images. Sometimes there are overtones that a reader can only be aware of but not be able to elaborate in words. From the angle of appreciating literature we can see the constant change in the way that people comprehend poems. In that regard, the standard for "faithfulness" based on understanding is impossible to remain the same all the time.

Besides, poetry translation faces greater challenges than translation in other genres in two aspects: the translation-resistance of the language and of the culture. English and Chinese are different tremendously in sentence, word, pronunciation and expression. English is a language of spelling with letters, but Chinese is a language of square characters with pictograph and ideograph. These factors lead not only to the difference in the superficial formation of the two languages but also a difference in the structure in depth of the two languages. In addition to the differences literature is an art of language but poetry is even more deeply involved in the art of language. Comparatively speaking Chinese classical poetry requires the greatest efforts to gain the extreme aesthetics of language. The cultural background of English-speaking countries is completely different from the cultural background of China. The different cultural backgrounds can also make literary works resistant to translation.

Facing these severe challenges and the narrow channel the cause of translating Chinese classical poems into English must make its own choice to abandon seeking after the reproduction of the form of poetry and the form of the language. Thus, it is possible to present the aesthetic perception nourished by Chinese culture. Song Qi said: "Literary works, particularly the first-rate works, are usually the fruits of great mental efforts. It is the responsibility of the translator to relay the abstract terms, such as the meaning and the state attained, the style of the author in handling the language, the mood that can only be perceived but not expressed and the tremendous spirit." [①] The kernel of this comment is to stress relaying the meaning and presenting the mood.

There is no doubt that it is painful to make such a decision. Chinese classical poems are dazzling treasures in the traditional Chinese culture. They are beyond any comparison in the world. Readers are so obsessed with its form and language of Chinese classical poetry that it may be hard to give them up. People are proud of the poems which are so live but void, full of images, with genuine feelings and a strong sense of harmony and tranquility. However, when we translate Chinese classical poems we are supposed to be rational and to take the following into our consideration: What is the purpose of translating them. The purpose is to show our best treasure to English- speaking people all over the world. And it's not for the native-language-speaking people to enjoy but for English-speaking people to enjoy. The specifics of translating Chinese classical poems

---

① Song Qi (Lin Yiliang), *Some Literary Works Selected as Examples*, Chinese University of Hong Kong Press, 1983.

into English are not the same as in translating English classical poems into Chinese. As most of English words have two or more syllables and all Chinese words have only one syllable, in translating English classical poems into Chinese there is much more room to take care of the rhythm and rhyme of the original English poem. But it is different when translating Chinese classical poems into English. The language in Chinese classical poems is always concise and succinct, in favor of using allusive quotations, strict in keeping with the patterns of rhythm and rhyme, and full of tonal patterns. All the above have created a very difficult task which is almost impossible to accomplish in the English language by translators. For a long time we have been laying more emphasis on the study of translation from English into Chinese, but luckily in recent years, there has been an upsurge in the study of translating Chinese classical poems into English. It is unfortunate that over stressing the concept of loyalty to the form and language of the Chinese classical poetry has prevailed. This is the bondage that slows down the cause of translating Chinese classical poems into English.

The translation of Chinese classical poems promotes the understanding of Chinese traditional culture, which makes it well known in the world and an influence on world literature. Professor Zhao Yiheng, a well-known scholar did a detailed academic analysis of this literary phenomenon in his book *The Muse From Cathay* —

The Influence of Chinese Classical Poetry on the New Poetry Movenment in America. [1] With great details and samples he shows how and to what degree Chinese classical poetry influenced the New Poetry Movement in America. His contribution in illustrating the influence is outstanding. On top of that his remarks on the translation of Chinese classical poems into English are penetrating, by pointing out the symptoms of damage to the original by adhering to a certain pattern of format and rhyme. In particular, his comments on the translation of Chinese classical poems into English free verse are brilliant. American poet Ezra Pound, a very important member of the New Poetry Movement predicted the tremendous influence of Chinese classical poems on the twentieth century American poetry. [2] Another important member of the American New Poetry Movement, Marianne Moore simply believed the new poetry was from Chinese classical poetry. [3]

If we take a look at those translations of Chinese classical poems, which had impact on the American New Poetry Movement in early twentieth century and on the poetry writing after 1950s in America and Britain it is quite likely that those poems were not

---

[1] Zhao Yiheng, *The Muse from Cathay — The Influence of Chinese Classical Poetry on the New Poetry Movenment in America,* Sichuan People's Publishing House, 1985.

[2] *Poetry,*1959(2):227.

[3] *New Poetry since 1912, Anthology of Magazine Verse,* 1926, p.1174.

translated in the same form of the original poem and not in the same language pattern of the original poem. The only explanation for this phenomenon is that the form of the Chinese classical poems was no longer in use at the beginning on twentieth century and all the rules for rhythm and rhyme did not exist in the modern Chinese poetry at that time. A large number of Chinese readers today as native speakers can only understand the Chinese classical poems by relying on translation into contemporary Chinese language plus notes. Meanwhile, the traditional pattern of rhythm and rhyme in English poetry had also been abandoned, particularly after the New Poetry Movement prevailed at the beginning of twentieth century. Sometimes you may still come across a few English poems written in the traditional form, but they are very rare. Of course, the change in English poetry writing could not be as thorough as the change in Chinese poetry writing because Chinese language itself was reformed and was turned into a modern language, which led to a complete elimination of the traditional form of poetry.

The nature of translation is to pass on information — content and aesthetics. Therefore, the issue in translating Chinese classical poems into English is how to focus on the transfer of the insightful aesthetics. The external aesthetics of Chinese classical poems — the form of the poem and the language, basically the rhyme and the rhythm — once were very functional. The pity is that this type of musical quality cannot be reproduced in an English translation.

Some translators try to present the rising and falling tones of a Chinese character through an application of the iambic metrical foot and the trochee metrical foot in English poetry; and also try to match the small number of characters in a verse line in Chinese classical poems by controlling the number of accented syllables in an English verse line; they even try to correspond the rhyming patterns in Chinese classical poems with the increasing of the rhyme in English translation of poems, and so on. Obviously, those efforts are wasted because those solutions were only to gain similarity, not the original form of the poem and the language. To be similar is not equal to being identical. When we say it is roughly the same form as in the original it is not yet the same. When we say it is roughly the same pattern of rhyme as in the original it is not yet the same. As a humorous story goes, a teacher asks children to guess how many legs an ostrich has. All the kids say four except one who says three. That kid gets the award because his answer is closer to the fact.

There is a concern that if we translate Chinese classical poems into English free verse target language readers would get a wrong concept that they are just like prose explaining the meaning of words. Nevertheless, it is still misleading if we translate them into a created form of similarity. On the other hand, the so-called prose or word-explanation in fact could be wonderful English free verse. If the translation of Chinese classical poems into English successfully produces the mood of art, the charm of art and the aesthetics of art it is a good one. It could be accepted by the English readers who may appreciate it and participate in recreation and enjoy the pleasure and to strengthen the interaction with poetry.

In the long history of art appreciation, the group of art admirers have established its orientation and psychology in art appreciation. In any case, translations of poems do not reach the standard of art appreciation, they will not be accepted. The theory that content and form in literature are unified and inseparable has been the cause of some failures. There is no doubt that some English readers have a hard time appreciating the translation of Chinese classical poems which still stick to the external form. They even doubt that the translations are really poems. It is extremely difficult for the translation of poems to succeed if the translators do not take the consciousness of the group of art admirers into serious consideration.

As a translator of Chinese classical poems, whose native language is Chinese, I always put the possibility for readers to appreciate the poem as the first consideration. When we translate English poems into Chinese, we know clearly what sort of form will be easily accepted while presenting the content and the aesthetics. On the contrary, when we translate Chinese classical poems into English we usually over stress the importance of keeping the aesthetics of form and we, otherwise, will feel ashamed in facing our ancestors. Yet you never know this is precisely the reason why the classical poems like clusters of glistening stars in the clear skies created by our ancestors seem dim and far away to foreign readers. Unfortunately, the translations of Chinese classical poems, that have great popularity abroad, have been held in contempt and considered unfaithful. However, the contribution those texts of translation have made is remarkable. To native speakers, the form of a poem is always helpful in presenting the internal aesthetics. But when we translate the poem into a language shaped by another culture we should adjust the original form to fit in a different culture. Otherwise the text of the translation will be rejected by the culture of the target language so that the purpose of the translation will have failed. I believe that in the original language the form and their content of poems are in harmony, but once the form is transferred into the culture of the target language without any adjustments the form and the content may be in conflict or even in confrontation. This is due to the choice of form and content made by the traditional culture in the original language, which is acceptable to the readers who were raised in the culture of the original language. The same content but in different culture can result in different aesthetic choices. Even the same content in the same culture may still result in different choices due to the variety of authors' cultural levels and artistical accomplishments or the variety of judgements regarding their readers. The unification of form and content is never an absolute necessity.

The fluctuation of change in contemporary poetry in Britain and America is a dazzling. If we refer to Longfellow we are out of date. There is no doubt about it. If we refer to Robert Frost we may still attract some readers, but there won't be many. That's for sure. Even Imagism vanished finally after some years of popularity. What we should refer to is contemporary poetry which has not only inherited the special qualities of previous schools of poetry but also has been constantly seeking for new creative poetry for new times. There is no need to worry about how long the text of the translation in contemporary style will be popular, as definitely there will be some new translators who will make new translations more cherished by readers in their time. That process is inevitable in history that any style will gradually be abandoned. In spite of this, history can be traced back and treasures can be found. If we give a broad view of trends in the history of translation, we discover that only those texts of translation appreciated by the group of art admirers at their time usually have ever-lasting value.

If the translation of a poem is not hindered by the obsession with external form the essence of the original poem — content and aesthetics will be revealed through translation. The external beauty serves only to expose the internal beauty and the existence of external beauty is only good for helping to expose the internal beauty. It is not hard to weigh advantages and disadvantages if we insist on being loyal to the form of the original and allowing the external form to become an obstacle for the exposure of the internal beauty. It is even worse to keep the external form and to display the beauty of the external form with the consequence that the negligence and damage to the internal aesthetics of the original do occur. It's very common that this kind of damage is hard to find, particularly hard for the target-language readers to figure out. Taking the advantage of this difficulty over-emphasizing the external form in translation of Chinese classical poems is openly promoted. Professor Li Xiyin wrote when he took the story about the Chinese word "weigh" as an example: "When we translate a work into another language we may happen to find out an amazing way to transfer indirectly the detailed characteristics of the original language. It is thrilling but 'It's not good to announce loudly and publicly, asking people to treat plum trees everywhere like this.' (Gong Zizhen 1792–1841). First, as every different language has its own different graceful characteristics, trying to treat all of them the same is not easy. If the translator doesn't have the adequate training the attempt to carve a swan may end up getting a duck. Second, translators may know this is tricky but still try hard to do it but somehow readers may not appreciate it." [1]

This issue is a serious issue in the field of translating Chinese classical poems and it is also common in the translation in other genres. I assume the point of view from the communication school is more practical in the international community of translation. They emphasize making the form of translation easier for the information recipients in the target language to understand and to appreciate. They stressed the important function of the information recipients — the target party in the procession of language communication. In other words, attention should be paid to making the readers in the target language get the stimulating effect of aesthetics and sympathetic response just as the readers of the original language would experience. While there is one thing I'd like to clarify that when we do the translation we can't just switch the cultural content with the cultural content of the target language. For example, the following English sentence: "It (something) is as significant (to me) as a game of cricket." should be translated into French like the following: "*C' estaussisignificant que de faire de la course de velo.*" (meaning "This is as significant to me as a bicycle race.") and should be translated into Chinese as "It is as significant to me as a magnificent feast." [2] In fact, this is not to get the translation text harmonised with

---

① Li Xiyin, "Thoughts on Translation," *Foreign Language Research,* 1987(2).

② Tan Zaixi and Eugene A. Nida, *Foreign Language Teaching and Research,* 1987(1).

the culture of the target language but to get the information content converted into the content in the culture of target language. In doing this, the translator has crossed the line and has exceeded the limit of a translator's right. Once the content created in the original is changed it is no longer translation but rewriting instead. If this logic is acceptable we may need to convert a blond beauty in the west into an image of black hair like dark clouds plus clear eyes and bright teeth in Chinese; and we may need to convert Sun Yat-sen into Washington; and we may need to know how we can convert dragon in that popular song *The Exponents of Dragon* since in Chinese dragon symbolizes prosperity, fortune and happiness but it symbolizes horror, cruelty and violence in English. This approach is not an attempt to establish a bridge between two languages and two cultures; instead it is crossing the line between the two different cultures and the two different languages to relay the meaning in the original. This will lead to the damage of meaning and will also block the channel for cultural fusion and for absorption of language from other cultures.

There is forever a limit in whatever we try to do. Provided we can master the limit we can build up the bridge through which we can pass on the insightful aesthetics and find out the connecting point between different languages and different cultures. The key point is to admit that there is no way in English to reproduce the external beauty of the Chinese classical poems because of the different culture, psychology and history reflected in the language. The only thing we can do is to fully expose the internal beauty of Chinese classical poems with English language. There is a story quoted often: a painter failed to create a beautiful Helen instead he created a wealthy Helen. When he was blamed he defended himself — There are limitations in the art of painting and I obey with respect the limitations so that I should be rewarded.[1]

Wang Shouyi

May 1986

Rewritten in September 1987

Rewritten in August 2018

Church Street, Toronto

Translated by Sun Suli, revised by Wang Shouyi

---

[1] Lessing G E, *The Laocoon and His Sons*, trans. Zhu Guangqian, People's Literature Publishing House, 1979.